Adam Andrews Johnson

1

THE MANTIS CORRUPTION

Acknowledgment

I want to extend my gratitude to all the guests who have joined us on the Book Slam podcast ☺ Each and every one of you marvelous authors is an inspiration! Thank you all for being part of my journey in writing.

Adam Andrews Johnson

5

This book is dedicated to Christa,
awaiting the destruction of the world.

Sumi and Harakin did not refer to their commander by his title. The two of them simply called him the *Voice*, and in the military compound where they were prisoners, his words were like an omniscient presence. They rarely saw him.

"Wake up, twins," said the Voice.

Sumi and Harakin were not twins. They were not the same age. The two were not even related, nor did they share the same skin color, but because neither of the women was human, *twins* was the term that stuck. There was disdain and dismissiveness when anyone in the skeleton crew of officers and medics at the compound said it, and for years, the two young women were referred to by the insult.

"Twins," the Voice repeated, "your commander orders you to be outside of the bunker in positions four and seven in 90 seconds."

Sumi and Harakin obeyed without question. They exited through the steel door that led out into the misty moorlands between the base and the great river. A moment later, they were in two separate locations, and they waited.

The dark of the night was quiet.

Sumi and Harakin knew what to do when the order was given.

"Engage," said the Voice.

Sumi disappeared and Harakin launched herself forward at a full-tilt run. The soles of her feet glowed, and they barely touched the ground. Sumi reappeared in the distance ahead of Harakin. She looked back at the other young woman who was running far faster than any human possibly could, and Sumi vanished again.

Their targets were not far.

Sumi stepped out of nothing and back into reality on the banks of the great river. She peered upstream through the darkness, and then down the river's opposite flow, but there were no signs of anyone or anything. No boat floated on this stretch of the river, and no houses lined its banks.

The houses that *did* sit close to the water's edge were not in sight, but they were not far. Sumi and Harakin were punished any time they went too near to the residences.

Then, there they were, the targets.

Sumi exited the world again, and she reentered it right in front of two naked men. Their bodies were bruised and bloody, and they were barefoot. They were racing through the soggy countryside like a pair of hunted rabbits, and the arrival of Sumi startled them so much that they both fell to the ground.

Terror was in their eyes, and they scrambled over each other to get up and try to run.

Harakin suddenly appeared with the flash from her illuminating feet and the glow of her vicious photon blades that protruded from each of her hands.

One of the naked men screamed, as Harakin collided with him and slashed with her light-knives. His arm was lopped off, went hurtling through the air, and it fell to the damp ground.

The other man watched in helpless horror, as Sumi grabbed his wrist, and she un-armed him as well. She stepped out of reality and took his forearm with her. His limb was simply gone.

Geysers of gore gushed from both men's severed stumps, but neither of the women was finished with their victims. The two weakened men tried to scramble away.

Sumi reappeared behind the man she had begun disassembling, and she placed her palm on his bare back. Again she left the world, and again she took a chunk of him with her.

He made a shrill noise, as his shoulder vanished into nothingness and his entire second arm flopped to the ground. He wheezed and coughed as the blood flowed from his missing limbs.

Sumi's next removal ended the man. She stepped through a doorway in reality and took his head.

As she disappeared again, the armless and headless corpse convulsed where it stood, and it crashed to the muddy soil.

Harakin's target was lumbering away from her. She swept her hands through the air and a flurry of countless tiny daggers of lumen energy impaled the man. He gurgled and collapsed to the sodden earth, and his blood pooled around his corpse.

Sumi and Harakin's task was always simple, to execute the victims put before them. There were rules, guidelines that needed to be followed, but their mission was always the same.

With the job completed, Sumi and Harakin returned to the base.

Ending lives became second nature for the two young women. Early in each of their imprisonments, both were forced to learn that *not* following orders came with horrible consequences. Being ignored for fulfilling their duties was preferable to the tortures used for punishment.

Sumi was first brought to the compound 15 years earlier. That was when her teleportation ability initially activated. She was only 9 years old at the time. For her initiation ceremony, the young girl was led into a chamber that contained six people tied to chairs lined up in a row. The prisoners were barely conscious, and each was badly beaten. Sumi was positioned in front of the first seated man.

"Kill him," commanded the Voice.

This was the first time Sumi heard him speak.

Before she could even respond to the order, an officer slit the throat of the prisoner at the other end of the row of chairs.

Sumi watched in shocked horror, as the man's blood flowed down his front like a gory waterfall. A moment later, he slumped forward, dead.

"Kill him," the Voice repeated.

Sumi did not know how to kill a person, and when she again did nothing, the officer stepped closer. There was no stop to the slow march of oncoming death. Despite Sumi's screams of protest, the other prisoners were slain one after another as the child wailed, and the officer drew closer to her with each kill. Tears streamed down Sumi's cheeks, but her terrified eyes stared. She could not look away from the slaughter. In a matter of brutal moments, only the bound man in front of Sumi was still living.

The other five corpses were each in a terrible state.

The Voice spoke again. "That man before you is going to die, whether you do it or not," and the prisoner whimpered. "If you do not kill him," the Voice continued, and he paused, "well, you're not going to like it."

The officer then stepped up to Sumi and loomed over her. He growled, snatched her shirt, and wiped the blood from his blade all over it.

"Last chance," warned the Voice.

The officer grabbed the final prisoner by the top of his head, and he stabbed his blade into one of the man's eyes; he let out a muffled scream into the gag.

Sumi could do naught but shriek.

The officer yanked his knife out, and he stuck it into the man's other eye.

The Voice cooed to young Sumi, "Kill the prisoner," as if he were offering her candy. "Put him out of his misery. My men can make his suffering last for a long, *long* time."

Sobs wracked the young girl's tiny frame, as the horrors of it overwhelmed her. She collapsed to the floor.

"Kill him," the Voice urged her in a sickly-sweet tone.

Sumi was forced to watch, as the man was stabbed in both of his arms and both of his legs. He screamed, and Sumi screamed, and the Voice laughed.

"Looks like we will have to do this all again tomorrow," the Voice said. "You'll have a lot of time to think about it tonight."

The officer pulled up the final prisoner's bloody shirt, and he slit the man across his stomach. His guts sloughed out and splattered onto the floor in front of Sumi.

She was pulled to her unsteady feet and dragged to a deeper part of the compound. The 9 year old girl was brought to a dark cell with a foul, putrid reek. Even the hallway to the chamber was barely lit, and the weak light did nothing to reveal what was in the darkness of the cell.

Sumi was pushed inside. The floor felt slimy and crunched under her little feet. All through the night, she screamed and cried, and she swatted at things that landed on her or crawled up her skin.

Her burgeoning ability to open doorways in reality had only teleported Sumi from one place to another by her line of sight, and she was trapped in the creeping darkness.

The following morning, in the glow of the rising sun, she was brought outside and hosed clean. Sumi was fed, but afterward, she was brought back to the execution chamber. Four more prisoners were tied to chairs. The scrawny child was powerless to fight against the officers who forced her in front of a tied and beaten woman.

A knife was placed in Sumi's hand. She had not been given one the day before.

"Kill her," the Voice commanded. "Unless you'd like another night with your new friends."

The officer sucked air through his teeth and made a chittering sound. He put his own knife's blade against the throat of the prisoner in front of him.

"Kill her."

The woman who Sumi was being ordered to kill moaned into the gag. Tears streamed from her eyes, and she pulled against the bonds but they held her fast.

Sumi began hyperventilating, and her terror from the crawling dark of the night before caused her to obey. The little girl stuck the blade into the woman's stomach.

"Good, *good!*" the Voice said with a wicked chuckle. "That wound will kill her slowly. It'll make for a good lesson. You can watch her suffer and see the life seep out of her. She will die in terrible pain," the Voice added. He almost sounded gleeful.

Sumi looked into the prisoner's eyes, as she pulled the blade out, and she stabbed the woman again. The little girl stabbed her over and over, sobbing and wailing as the Voice laughed. After what felt like an eternity to Sumi, the woman was dead.

The child received no prize or reward for fulfilling the horrible task that was set before her, but that night, she was *not* locked in the vile cell. She learned to kill without question, or face the creeping darkness.

Sumi spent the following nine years, nine soul-crushing and mind-numbing years, nine seemingly endless years alone in training. In that time, the officers taught her how to fight, and Sumi's human captors took great pleasure in defeating their non-human prisoner in practice combat. They would jump her when she was not expecting it and leave her beaten, sometimes badly. By the time she was 18 years old, Sumi was hardened like granite. Her nose was crooked from being broken many times, and her hands were almost always balled into fists. She was wary of every encounter with the officers or the medics.

Sumi was taught how to use her powers of teleportation to access and enter places from which she was barred. She was also taught to use her unique ability to kill. She trained herself to disconnect from the actions demanded of her, to the point that she would slaughter any prisoner put in front of her outright.

The Voice began sending her out on missions. Since Sumi could get into anywhere, she became a regular member of the kill-squads. At the base, killing was her primary requirement, but she was rarely made to kill in the field. Her task was always to get the mercenaries into wherever their targets were hiding.

One night, without warning, she was sent on unexpected exercises. A squad led her past the compound's obstacle course and out into the rolling lands that surrounded the base. They brought her to the perimeter of the capital city, but at no point that night was she required to use her teleportation.

At sunrise, the group made it back to the base, and she was permitted to return to the dormitory. Sumi was surprised to find a young girl asleep in one of the beds. It had been so many years that Sumi was the only youth, that for a moment, she just stood there and stared at the child. She tried to quietly change out of her mission gear, but the girl sat up with a bleary expression.

Seeing the child sparked something in Sumi. It was not that she never saw other children, she often crossed paths with the capital's homeless rabble while out on missions, but this girl was like *her*; the child was not human. There was a pale illumination coming from her skin. Sumi was experiencing an emotion that she was not used to, and it was like a glittering fleck of quartz crystal revealed in the granite that had become her soul.

Sumi spent very little time talking to others. When the dark moments of her life at the compound were at their worst, she would talk to her faded memories, or even just the walls of her lonely home. There were many dark moments in that place.

"Hi," she said to the girl.

The child looked at Sumi with an unfocused gaze, and she fell back against the pillow into unconsciousness.

Sumi's eyes stayed fixed on the sleeping girl, as she finished changing. She climbed into her own bed and soon fell asleep with the morning sun beginning to brighten the room.

It was early in the afternoon when she awoke, and the dormitory was again empty, but the bed that the girl slept in was disheveled. Sumi went to the door and turned the handle.

It was locked. The door was never locked.

Sumi knew that she was not permitted to leave the compound, and even if she did, there was nowhere she could go. She also knew it was impossible for her to be accepted anywhere, but locking the door was asinine; locked doors were her power's specialty. Even though Sumi could have been on the other side of the door in an instant, she remained in the room out of spite.

There was a plate of food on the table, and she started to eat her bland breakfast.

Hours later, Sumi awoke on the cold uncomfortable floor.

It was already dark outside.

She pushed herself upright.

The officers had locked her in a room that they *knew* could not hold her, but then they also drugged her food. They had never drugged her before. Sumi pulled herself up into the chair with her head spinning. She tried to be angry at her captors for this new treatment, but her brain refused to focus, and it was several minutes before she was able to gather herself.

Sumi barely remembered her previous life, the life before she was snatched from her home and taken to the compound. Nine lonely years dragged by in that horrible place, and her time there almost completely overshadowed, or made her forget whatever childhood she had experienced. Sumi often tried to hone in on her vague memories, back from a time when she was not used as a living weapon.

Her brain felt foggy, but she suddenly remembered the child and looked over at the bed. The girl was again asleep under the covers, and quite a few objects were now beneath the bedframe, including a large trunk and some toys.

Sumi was brought to the compound without a single possession. She pushed herself to her unsteady feet, walked over to the sleeping girl, and reached down to pick up a stuffed animal. A bell on its hat jangled.

The child groaned and opened her eyes. She sat up and looked at Sumi.

"Where's mama?" she asked, and she started to cry.

Her tears quickly became uncontrolled sobbing, and the inexperienced 18 year old did not know what to do. Sumi looked around, but the Voice did not speak. It did not give any instructions or guidance, nor did it rattle in her ears about her duty. It did not even crackle on noisily to tell her the child's name. The Voice remained silent.

Sumi stepped up next to the bed, put her hand on the child's back, and the girl wrapped her arms around Sumi's waist.

She wailed.

Eventually, exhaustion calmed the child, and Sumi said in a soft voice, "My name's Sumi. What's yours?"

The girl rubbed her eyes, sniffed hard, and said, "Harakin."

"Your name is Harakin?" Sumi confirmed, testing the name, and the girl nodded. "Where do you come from, Harakin? Where were you before you came to this place?"

A sob choked the child, but she managed to say, "I was with mama and dada and bobo. We were at the waterfall. Then some bad men came," and the girl started to cry again.

"Did they hurt you?" Sumi asked. She was uncertain in her actions and clumsily ran her fingers over the girl's hair.

Harakin shook her head *no*.

"They didn't hurt you, okay, good. Did they hurt your family?" Sumi whispered, but again the child indicated that they did not. "I don't understand, Harakin," she said in a gentle voice. "What happened? What did they do to you?"

"Mama and dada let the men take me away," Harakin whimpered. "They didn't want me anymore, and they let them take me. They didn't take bobo, but they took me." She broke down again in pitiful, body-shaking sobs. Sumi could not calm her, and the girl cried until she fell back to sleep.

The drugs were still making Sumi's head spin, and she staggered across the room. She clambered onto her bed, sat upright, and hugged her knees to her heart. She closed her eyes, rested her forehead against her thighs, and tried to dredge up any memory from her time before the compound.

The next day, Sumi and Harakin were both roughly awakened at dawn. They were shoved down the hallway that led to the execution chamber. Within the room, seven prisoners were tied to chairs in a row. Two of them were beaten so badly they were unconscious.

Sumi instantly knew what was happening. She looked at little Harakin, as the child was pushed to one end of the seated prisoners.

For the briefest moment, Sumi hesitated.

The officer grabbed Sumi by the shirt and yanked her close to his face. His breath stank as he made his wicked insect noise at her.

She cringed away from him, and the man released his grip on her clothes. Sumi looked back at Harakin again, as if to apologize, then she stepped up to the other end of the row of bound prisoners.

By only 18, Sumi had already executed too many people to count. She told herself that these prisoners now before her were just more of the same, but she knew it was a lie when the officer unsheathed his knife. He extended it to her, and her mind went numb, as her fingers wrapped around the hilt. Killing humans was so easy with her powers. She simply needed to open one of her eldritch doorways and teleport a piece of her target into nothing.

Sumi looked down at the knife in her hand. She knew what was expected of her.

The Voice spoke to Harakin in his most tempting tone.

"Kill him," he oozed.

Just like nine years earlier, when Sumi was first ordered to execute a prisoner, Harakin was not given a knife or anything else that she could have used to kill someone. This brutal ceremony was meant to terrorize her, meant to reveal to her the world of which she was now a part. It was meant to set the tone for the rest of her existence, and the human captors liked their tortures of the non-human living weapons.

In Sumi's mind, she was thrust back to her initiation. She knew the punishment for failing to fulfill her duty. Over her years of imprisonment, Sumi spent countless nights in the dark cell. Sometimes she was locked in for resisting an order, sometimes for no other reason than to keep her spirit broken.

Sumi took a breath, stared at the tied person in front of her, and she gritted her teeth. In one fell swipe, she slit the prisoner's throat. Sumi squinted her eyes shut against Harakin's scream of horror. The child bawled and cried, and tears trickled from Sumi's eyes, but she did what she knew was required of her.

She also knew full well that Harakin could not escape being put in the dark cell for the night; the threat of being locked in it was constant at the compound, and the smothering of hopes and dreams was the goal. All the fears that Sumi felt for the horribleness within the cell forced her to do to Harakin, the same thing that was done to her those long years ago.

The screaming girl was again instructed by the Voice to kill the chained man before her, as Sumi took a step closer.

She looked at the next person in front of her, and all the while Harakin wailed. One by one, the 18 year old continued to slaughter the other prisoners, while drawing nearer to Harakin.

Sumi stabbed one man in the jugular and a massive gush of blood showered the prisoner tied beside him. She jabbed the knife multiple times into the lungs and hearts of the next two bound people. The following individual's throat was slit, and then Sumi stepped up beside Harakin.

The child looked small and frail.

Five prisoners were dead.

The Voice laughed.

In front of Sumi was a woman tied to a chair, and she was about to cut her throat, when the Voice interrupted.

"Show her," he commanded.

The officer reached toward Sumi, and she gave him back his bloody blade.

Sumi looked at Harakin, took a shallow breath, and then she brought her palm to the gagged woman's chest.

The prisoner gazed up at Sumi with hope, feeling the soft touch of a gentle hand that no longer held a weapon.

Then Sumi's entire body blinked.

The woman gasped in shock, as a giant cavity the size of a grapefruit opened in her torso beneath Sumi's palm. All of the flesh and bones and organs in the space that existed a moment ago were gone. The woman jerked in her chair as her innards bulged out of the opening, and she slumped forward, dead. A gruesome river of slime and blood poured down her body and splattered on Harakin's feet.

The child coughed and hacked and vomited onto the floor of the execution chamber. She did not comprehend what she witnessed, and nothing could overshadow her all-encompassing terror.

"Kill him," the Voice instructed young Harakin in a tone dripping with poisonous sweetness. "Kill him."

She could not.

Sumi balled her fingers into a fist that she squeezed with all her might, trying to build herself up for what she was expected to do. She took the knife back from the officer, looked at the final living prisoner, and she stuck the blade into his stomach.

He grunted in pain and ground his teeth into the gag.

Sumi left the knife in him and took her hand away. She paused, then she reached forward and gripped the hilt. In an instructive way, she twisted the blade, pulled it out, and stuck it back into the man. Again, she left it in him. Tears leaked from her eyes as she tortured the prisoner for her captors, but she dared not leave the task incomplete. The prisoner groaned as Sumi repeated her action, wrapping her fingers around the handle, and the blade slid out of the man, red and glistening. Then, again, she stabbed it back into him. His wounds seeped blood down his legs.

"Kill him," the Voice hissed to Harakin.

He whimpered, as Sumi showed Harakin over and over how to stab someone. The man was pierced many times, as Harakin cried and screamed.

Sumi's tears also flowed freely, and she continued to stab the man in his torso until the life left his eyes and he fell still.

"Show her again," demanded the Voice.

Sumi handed the knife to the officer and placed her palm against the corpse's forehead. It was almost as if a flash of light emanated from her, but there was no illumination, as her entire body blinked again. Sumi disappeared from reality through one of her doorways, and she returned to it in the same instant. However, the man's head was gone.

Blood oozed from the hideous hole of his neck.

At only 11 years old, Harakin did not understand her powers. She was grabbed by the officers and dragged from the room.

Sumi stood still, painfully aware of how ineffectual she was at protecting this new child, and yet internally begging to be ignored by the officers. She was also silently screaming for them to leave Harakin alone, but she stood resolute and obedient.

A moment later, Sumi was by herself with the seven dead bodies. She wished there was some way to save Harakin from the crawling dark of the punishment cell, and Sumi felt guilty about her gratitude that she was being left alone. She returned to the dormitory.

Day slowly became night, and Sumi knew the child was still suffering in the darkness. She hated that she could not save her from the compound and the horrible people who ran it, but she could not even save herself.

Sumi spent that night buried in memories from before her life at the compound, memories she was no longer certain were real. Even if they were only fantasies, those thoughts allowed her to escape into her mind.

The following day, she was awakened by the sounds of commotion. She rose, approached the window, and saw young Harakin outside in the morning sun. The filth from the cell was being hosed off of her, and several guards were jeering and laughing. Sumi knew the water was cold.

Harakin was returned to the dorm, and she was shaking to her bones.

"Are you..." Sumi started to ask, and Harakin turned toward her.

"*You're a monster!*" the girl shrieked. "Stay away from me!"

Whatever interactions Sumi had experienced with other children during her youth long ago were forgotten, and she did not know how to respond to the girl, so she vanished.

Harakin was left standing alone in the empty communal bedroom, sobbing and hopeless and cold.

Sumi stepped back into the world at the only location to which she could escape.

The rusted remains of an old six-story watchtower loomed over the compound. Its ladders deteriorated decades earlier, but the platform at the top was still stable. No one could access the upper landing except for Sumi, and no one knew that she sometimes hid on the old skeleton of a structure when life at the base got to its lowest.

She sat on the sun-scorched planks and stared out toward the distant spires that sparkled on the horizon. As horrible as her life was at the compound, Sumi knew that she did not belong with the humans who dwelt in that far-off city; she knew that she did not fit in with them.

She thought back over the long years. The officers had forced her to kill more people than she could count. They trained her to use her unusual abilities, how to access her powers at will, and how they could be harnessed to kill.

Sumi knew what the future held for Harakin, and a terrible idea flashed into her mind. She considered killing the child, putting the girl out of her misery before the inevitable happened to her, but Sumi knew she could not do it. The countless masses that she had executed over her nine years were each a part of her survival in that brutal place. Killing Harakin would be a different kind of killing.

The breeze was warm, and Sumi dropped her head to her hands and sobbed. She grieved the life that was stolen from her all those years ago, and she mourned for Harakin over the inevitable suffering that was to come.

Sumi stayed on the lookout for many hours that day. The ever-present Voice did not speak, did not demand her appearance or her presence, and she remained alone until sundown.

When she returned to the dorm, the child was again gone, and a plate of grey food was waiting for her. Sumi was hungry but wary of the tasteless meal. However, after she finished eating, nothing happened. The food was not drugged.

Then the door opened. Harakin was shoved into the room. She fell to her knees, bawling pitifully, and the door slammed behind her. Harakin was covered in blood.

Sumi put some warm water in a bowl and grabbed a few rags. She knelt beside Harakin and began to clean the gore from the girl.

Harakin wailed, but she did not resist.

No words were needed in that moment, and Harakin's shuddering sobs filled the quiet of the room. Sumi wiped away much of the blood, then helped the child remove her sticky clothes, and led her into one of the shower stalls.

Harakin continued to whimper, as the warm water cleansed away the gore on the outside of her, but it did nothing to remove the misery that was now her life. When she was clean, she calmed down, and Sumi tucked her into bed.

Then she lay down beside young Harakin, and Sumi tried to remember what her mother did when she was upset all those years ago. She knew that no bad thing from Harakin's previous life could possibly compare with what awaited her, and Sumi put one arm over the child. It felt like a pathetic attempt to make up for the incalculable villainy into which Harakin was thrust, but together, they fell asleep.

Harakin quickly realized Sumi was not a monster, and that they were prisoners *together* in that vicious place.

Six grueling years dragged by, and despite the officers' attempts to pit them against one another, the two non-humans formed a bond that was closer than sisterhood. They were not twins, and although the term was used as an insult, *twins* was very much what the two of them felt like.

Sumi found herself locked in the dark cell far more frequently over those six years. She often took the blame and subsequent punishment for things that would have gotten Harakin sent to the darkness. Despite Sumi's time spent killing, a tiny recess in her heart flickered with the sparks of compassion and empathy. They were like those memories that she could not even be certain were real, but that she clung to nonetheless. She cared for Harakin, and even though their human captors treated both of them horribly, Sumi was able to tap into some long-forgotten kindness.

Life at the compound was brutal, and soon Harakin was also killing on command. During those six years, she was trained to access her unique abilities, and the officers forced her to use them to kill.

Sumi and Harakin's powers were very different, but under the guidance of cruel men, each was used as a weapon. The two were destined to be prisoners at the compound until the day they died, but their next assignment would push them beyond their limits and was to be the beginning of their liberation.

They were sent to kill a king★

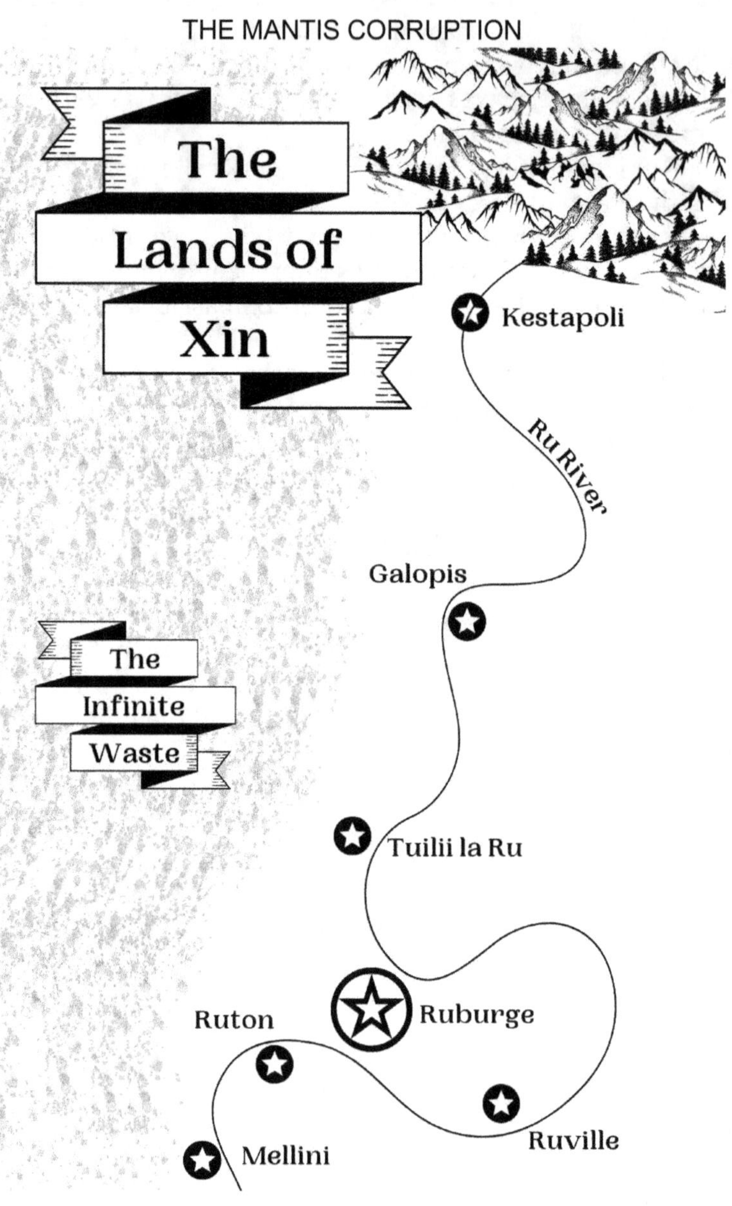

Chapter 2 – Tisa and the Witch, Part One

The natural northern border to the land of Xin was formed
by a mighty mountain range, and from those craggy peaks ran a

powerful river, the Ru. Long ago, the water carved its path that snaked through the western region for hundreds of miles. Several villages dot the banks on its journey south, and the river provides an abundance of fish for the people, as well as a means of transportation. To the east, a vast region of rolling hills and dales stretches to the sea, but in the wastes beyond the Ru River, there is only death.

Far to the north, in the shadow of the mountains sits the village of Kestapoli. It straddles the Ru River where its waters first reach the flatlands, and a portion of the village is located on either of the river's banks. Kestapoli is the smallest town of Xin and the greatest distance from the capital. Rapids rage upstream, but the village is positioned at a bend where the river becomes calm and placid. The two separate sides of Kestapoli are very similar, with cafes and taverns along the waterfront, and residences set back behind them.

Just upriver outside of Kestapoli lived a woman who the villagers referred to as the witch of the whitewater. They thought of her as a feral hag who did not belong anywhere except on the outskirts of society. Her hovel was little more than a cave, one she dug for herself beneath the roots of a great old tree beside the churning rapids. Her hair and skin were always caked in mud, and she kept herself wrapped in strange scaly material. She could occasionally be seen talking to the trees or even shouting at them.

People from Kestapoli visited the witch of the whitewater from time to time, for it was rumored that she could see the future. Later, when they were a safe distance from her, back in the village, they whispered that her mind was broken from knowing too much. Some claimed that she was hundreds of years old. It was even said that the priestesses of Ruburge far to the south once came to her for the eldritch wisdom she possessed.

Youths sometimes dared each other to see who could creep closest to her dwelling, before fleeing in terror and giggling to shake away their fear. During the high festival of the spring equinox, some of the little Kestapoli girls and boys dressed themselves in rags and pretended to be the witch of the whitewater. They disheveled their faces and hair and bodies with leaves and mud. Then they chased the other children, and whoever was caught needed to give the make-believe witch a sunberry in order to continue playing the game.

THE MANTIS CORRUPTION

Sunberries grew wild all across the northern region of Xin, and on the rare occasion when a villager went to visit the witch, they brought her some of the little red fruits, which she loved and ate constantly. Their juices were thick, and every equinox, the children would have stained fingers by the end of the celebrations. The witch's lips were permanently crimson.

Tisa was only 13 years old the first time she visited the witch.

The grimy woman was seated on the dirt of the forest path as Tisa approached her home beneath the tree. Out of sight, the rapids roared; the river was close. This region of the forest was rocky. Huge boulders were strewn through the trees, as if giants had thrown them around long ago. Compared to the grasslands, the area felt magical to Tisa, and it added to the witch's mystery.

She was staring right at Tisa as she rounded the bend in the trail, as if the witch knew that the child was on her way. Of course, that was why Tisa was there; the witch knew the future. However, nothing could have prepared the girl for the unusual appearance of the woman.

"You ain't gonna like the answers," she hissed before Tisa said a word.

The witch was thick, a stocky and muscular woman with broad shoulders and strong thighs. Physically, she was angular, and her jaw was like a brick. Her mussed appearance gave her a chaotic quality that made her seem animalistic, and her red-stained lips were strange-looking. When the witch smiled, she looked crazed.

Tisa thought to herself that the witch did not even appear to be all that old.

The woman stood, and things became more shocking for Tisa.

Her full height was about the same as the girl's, but there was more to her form than that of a human. Tisa tried to hold in her surprise, as the scaly material that the witch kept wrapped around her opened and revealed itself to be a pair of wings. They extended and spread behind her. The wings looked like they belonged to a mythical dragon, but they looked heavy and Tisa thought that they did not seem to provide the witch with flight.

Beneath the mud that obscured the color of her hair and caked her skin, she was naked, and Tisa was surprised to realize that almost every inch of her was covered in strange markings. They were not simply discolorations, but instead, Tisa could see three-dimensional ripples of textured skin.

The witch was wearing what might be described as jewelry. Skulls from many animals were strung on a necklace that draped down between her bare breasts. Bones were tied to her fingers and forearms, and there were even some tangled in her hair.

She turned and waved for Tisa to follow her, and as she walked, her wings synchronized with her legs and swept forward and back with each step. The witch nodded to Tisa and entered the muddy hollow beneath the tree.

Tisa sucked air through her teeth. The game of being dared to sneak toward the witch's house was a far cry from standing at the doorway, ready to enter. She looked back over her shoulder in the direction of Kestapoli, but Tisa knew that she needed the witch's wisdom, and she entered.

"You ain't gonna like it," the witch said again in a singsong voice. She reached over her shoulder to one of her wings, took hold of a single scale, and gritted her teeth. One sharp yank tore the scale free, and the witch rolled her eyes, as a tiny trickle of blood dribbled down from the self-inflicted wound.

She looked at Tisa and chuckled malevolently. "It's bad news."

Tisa furrowed her brow and asked her question. "How do I die?" she demanded. It was not the question that was truly plaguing her mind, but she had not formulated that one completely.

"Horribly," the witch replied.

"I already expected that," Tisa responded in a confident tone. She was nonplussed by the woman's dramatics. "When, where, why, how? What else can you tell me?"

"But you're already so old," the witch said to the 13 year old girl. "You don't need to know those things. The information will arrive soon enough, even without your knowing it."

Tisa gasped. "So, it's going to happen soon?"

"You're already dead and you just don't know it yet."

Tisa scowled. She was not afraid of the witch, unlike everyone else who *was*. "I'm not dead," she retorted.

"You're dead, and I am fresh and clean in a holy place where I don't want to be." Suddenly the witch screamed, *"And it's all your fault!"*

Tisa staggered back.

The witch stuck the wing-scale into her mouth, gulped it down with a drink from a mug of foamy green liquid, and she became motionless. Her gaze was down on the floor by her feet.

Tisa waited.

Nothing happened.

Within the quiet stillness of the witch's home, moisture condensed and dripped with tiny splashes onto the floor.

Then the woman raised her head, and her features were gone, replaced with many glowing eyes that covered her entire face. The eyes simultaneously looked right, then up, left, and finally down. In unison, all the eyes blinked, but when they reopened, each was a bright white void.

Tisa was breathless. A tear even welled in one eye, as she beheld a being with such radiance, that it could only be described as *beauty*. This woman was not frightening, as Tisa's fellow villagers thought; she was magnificent.

The witch's body became rigid and she remained motionless, as a voice emanated from her mouthless form.

"You will die after killing many," she began. "You will die in agony surrounded by suffering masses. You will die by accident. You will die in pieces, like the pieces of others you will create. Your questions are answered," the witch concluded, but her face of eyes remained.

Tisa frowned. "What questions? Those answers didn't tell me anything that I wanted to know, and I'm not even sure what you thought you were answering. I haven't even asked you anything except how I die."

"Yes, and all four of your questions are answered."

Tisa frowned. She knew what she needed to do, and she closed her eyes. In the air between her and the witch, a hole opened like a void in reality. Tisa caused a black flower to rise from it. It bloomed, then it disappeared along with the void.

"Now do you understand why I came to see you?" Tisa asked.

The witch's many eyes continued to glow with light that did not illuminate the cave, and she replied, "I knew why you were coming here before I was born."

Much of what the woman said made no sense to Tisa.

"I'm one of them," Tisa declared. She then asked in a quiet voice, "What am I supposed to do?" Her question may have been rhetorical, but the witch responded to her.

"The hunted, nature's forsaken, *Shifts* some folks call us."

"*Us?*" Tisa asked. "I knew it! You're one, too, aren't you?"

The witch stretched out her arms and her heavily-scaled wings, and Tisa thought she should feel awkward with the naked woman standing in front of her. However, the strange markings that twisted all over the witch's skin were mesmerizing, even beneath the layer of grime; Tisa could not look away from her.

"There is a child who is the inverse of you," stated the witch. "The child is trapped." Her wings lowered, and the voice that came from her continued, "But first, *the I* must do that thing which *the I* has always avoided because *the I* was afraid. *The I* must see the time that *the I* has forever refused to look into, and in so doing, reveal all the truth of the universe to the self." The witch sighed. "And *the I* will be one."

Tisa was confused. "Be one what?" she asked. "The *eye?*"

"All time is exposed to *the I*, but there is one time that *the I* cannot look into until 'tis that time."

"Okay," Tisa said, not following the witch, "so how do I find the trapped child."

"The child has not yet been born."

Tisa scrunched up her face. "So, let me get this straight. You're not going to tell me anything useful about my death. You're talking nonsense about time, and now there's some kid who isn't even born yet," and Tisa hesitated, "but *someday* is going to get trapped somewhere?"

The witch did not reply, but her arms dropped, and she knelt down in the mud of her hollow and said, "You will not save the child." Her face full of eyes blinked. The light faded from them, and all but her two normal eyes vanished. She reached out, grabbed her mug, and took another swig of the green beverage.

Tisa groaned. "You'll never be clean, not living here." She stepped up to the witch and scratched a flaky bit of dried mud off her cheek. "What's your name?" Tisa asked.

The witch responded in a gruff deep voice, as if she was trying to impersonate a man. "Monster," she stated.

"No," Tisa replied gently, "not the things people have called you. What's your real name?"

"*Harbinger of wickedness!*" the witch yelled.

Tisa tried to console her. "Calm down. No one is going to hurt you."

"The hideous whore!"

"Please," Tisa pleaded, "these things are not what you are!"

"Destroyer of dreams, hateful whisperer, pockmarked princess, the vilest visionary, sorceress of eyes, *witch of the whitewater!*" she screamed.

Tisa closed her eyes again, and she caused multiple voids to open in the air around the witch. From each, a little black flower extended, and the witch fell still, as she watched the blossoms grow.

"Be calm," Tisa whispered to her. "What do I call you?"

"Liovia," the witch replied. Her eyes were fixed on the flowers.

"Liovia?" Tisa repeated.

Over the following months, as the spring rains soaked the lands of Xin, Tisa worked on a project. Using her family's sledge, the 13 year old girl began hauling lumber into the forest toward the base of the mountains. In some ways, Tisa was still very childish, but the girl was already a skilled builder. She did not like foraging or hunting or gardening, but construction was a part of village life that she had loved ever since she was a young child.

Tisa was 4 the first time she helped her parents coat the outside of their home in pitch for the winter. She was 6 when she assisted installing new doors and windows. At only 9 years old, Tisa decided that the shed beside their house needed to be replaced, and under the supervision of her parents, she built a new one from scratch. Tisa did repairs to the family home as needed, and she was so enthusiastic about building, that no one in her family batted an eye when one day she started dragging wood and tools out into the forest.

By midsummer, Tisa had constructed a small hut beside the muddy hollow where the witch lived, and she continued her woodworking into the beginning of autumn. Tisa filled the new sturdy little shack with a bedframe, two chairs, and a small table. The days grew shorter as the season slipped closer to winter, but every time Tisa checked on the witch, she was still beneath her tree.

Even in the coldest winters, the temperature in northern Xin rarely approached freezing, and the snows remained high on the mountains. However, the witch's mud pit seemed inhospitable to Tisa, but Liovia refused to set foot into the hut she build for her.

"That's your house," the witch told Tisa one morning, and those three little words sparked something in the girl's mind.

That night, when she arrived back at her family's home, she told her parents, "On my next birthday, I'm moving out."

Her mother and father dismissed the notion as a passing fancy, but as midwinter and Tisa's birthday grew nearer, she reminded her parents of her intention.

This time, they paid attention.

"What do you mean *you're leaving*?" her mother asked in an incredulous tone.

Tisa's father initially seemed to be supportive. "Where will you go? Are you leaving alone? What are your plans after you leave Kestapoli? How will you feed yourself?" Then it became clear that he was not interested in her answers but just intended to dissuade her. "You don't have a source of income. You have no skills in the garden to grow food. You've let all your friendships fall by the wayside, and that boy who liked you still turns up from time to time, looking for you. You'll be 14 in a little over a week, it's almost time for you to start thinking about a family."

Tisa was appalled. It was true that some of the villagers coupled as early as the age of 15, but Tisa knew she was not meant for that life. She desperately wanted to tell her parents everything, and even more desperately wanted them to tell her that everything was going to be alright and nothing was changed. Tisa already knew she was so different that everything was going to change and nothing would be alright.

"I don't belong here," she told them. "I'm not like you."

Her mother scoffed. "You're our daughter," she huffed. "Of course, you belong here. Oh, wait a second," she sneered in a sarcastic tone. "I see! You've found some boy, haven't you? You found someone who you consider to be *not* one of our village idiots. Well, I refuse to let you go off and live like a tramp."

"What?!" Tisa squawked. "That's not it!"

The dichotomous suggestions of her father telling her to *settle*, and her mother telling her that she would do no such thing, were making Tisa's head spin with confusion. She needed to explain to them what her plans were, but her father spoke over her.

"No, I know what it is," he said with a scowl, "and I'm ashamed of myself for not stopping you. I know you've been taking wood to that witch. I should have forbidden you from visiting the old hag, once I realized what you were up to, but I…"

His voice vanished, as Tisa closed her eyes, and a multitude of little pockets of shadow opened in the air all around her. From the darkness within them rose little chubby figures.

They waved at her parents, and her parents each took a fearful step back.

"I'm different," Tisa stated in a timid but determined voice, "and I'm going to live at the base of the mountains."

"You can't be a…" her mother started, but she refused to use the word *Shift* and settled on, "one of *them*. Neither of *us* are," she added, looking at her husband. "Those things are not normal, they're… they're freaks! It's just not possible you were born that way."

Tisa's father pointed an accusatory finger at his daughter. "The witch has turned you into one of those abominations!" he yelled. "You are going to stay here and we will get that evil right out of you!"

This was not the way Tisa expected the conversation to go. Her parents were aware that unique individuals were sometimes born with incredible abilities; they were familiar with the witch. However, Tisa also knew that in Xin, the topic simply was not discussed. Her mother and father were always supportive of her, encouraging and loving, but they now showed a side that their daughter had never experienced before.

"You are a great disappointment," her father went on, "and you've shamed our family name. How dare you act like it's okay for you to spend your time around that monster? You are forbidden from ever seeing the witch of the whitewater again!"

"She's not a monster," Tisa pleaded. "Her name is Liovia. Please, just look at what I can do." She lowered her eyes adoringly to the little figures of darkness that surrounded her.

Things were already bad for Tisa, but they were about to get catastrophically worse.

Her mother grabbed the handle of a pot of boiling water from the stovetop, and she threw it at her daughter, as she shrieked, *"We'll purify you!"*

Tisa screamed as the water scalded her chest and upper arm. The metal pot collided with the front of her thigh, and it was so hot that even though it only touched her for a split second, Tisa's leg was also burned. The pain in her body was excruciating, like nothing she had ever felt in her entire young life, and she cowered away.

The hooded shadow characters from her void discs launched forward and swept across the room. Even through her pain, Tisa looked on in horror as they smothered her mother in chomping teeth of darkness. Tisa's mother screamed and flailed at the vaporous entities, as they removed chunk after gruesome chunk of her flesh. Tisa's father tried to brush the little biting monsters off of his wife, but his hands passed through them as if they were nothing more than shadow. Blood began to pool on the floor around Tisa's mother and her wailing was terrible.

Her parents were powerless to stop the creatures, as they devoured all ten of the woman's fingers and her toes. She shrieked in agony as they ate her ears and nose and lips, even her eyelids were chewed away, giving her a grisly and gristly expression. Her cries began to grow weak, and Tisa's father rose in shock from his wife's twitching body.

He grabbed a cleaver from the countertop and raised it above his head. His eyes were filled with madness as he turned on his daughter with the huge blade.

Tisa was terrified, and the shadow creatures leapt from her mother and swarmed her father. Instead of biting him, they morphed into little spikes that stabbed into the man's limbs and torso. He was punctured many times where he stood, and blood squirted from his body in every direction like a gruesome fountain. He did not scream, but he made little gurgling noises and fell to a clump on the floor. The cleaver landed beside him.

Tisa's shadows vanished.

She was bawling.

Her tears were already flowing at the pain of her burned flesh, but seeing her parents lying dead made her sob in misery. Long minutes she cried, then fear began to overshadow her sorrow, and Tisa fled her home and the village of Kestapoli.

She ran. With her head spinning and her blistered skin screaming at her, she ran. Under the shadow of the mountains, Tisa entered the trees where the edge of the forest began, and she did not stop running. She did not stop running until she collided with Liovia who was standing in the middle of the pathway.

Both of them fell to the ground, and Tisa exploded with sobs that wracked her frame.

The witch leaned over her and placed her palm on Tisa's back. "You don't feel the pain anymore," she told the child.

Liovia's words did not help Tisa's brutal agony, both outside and in. The pain of her scalded flesh was nothing compared to the crushing feelings in her soul. She did not know what happened, but she knew that her parents were dead.

Tisa entered the hut that she had built for Liovia, and the witch began to nurse the girl back to health.

In Kestapoli, several people talked about sending out a search party to look for Tisa. However, with the condition of the child's massacred parents, the villagers decided a search would be pointless. They assumed the girl could only be in a worse state than her parents. No one ever went looking for her.

Tisa stayed with the witch of the whitewater, and puberty progressed quickly for her. She soon grew tall and thin. There were rare instances when a villager from Kestapoli would bolster their courage and trek upriver to see the witch and her young acolyte, but none of them ever considered that the acolyte was Tisa. Most of the two women's time was spent without the company of anyone else.

As the years slipped by, Tisa got to know the northern forests of Xin better than anyone except maybe the witch. Not many people ventured into those dark woods.

On an unremarkable day that was very much like any other, Liovia informed Tisa, "*The I* must become one."✪

Chapter 3 – Gunge, Part One

Between the vast rolling plains of Xin and the mountains far to the north lies a narrow band of foothills that serves as a realm of monsters, a land of beasts. The twisted fiends who dwell therein are not part of normal society, and there they have made a vile home for themselves among the others who have chosen to slither the same villainous path. They call their region Gunge.

The inhabitants are few in number and there is no village in their region. The choices that they made in their past have limited their needs, and their physical bodies no longer require food or water. They have abandoned their human forms, adopting new and mutated visages of terror. There are no buildings on their land, and the creatures nest together in a grotesque mass of unnatural flesh. Like the enormous rat-king in *The Nutcracker*, in which the rodents had become tangled to one another's tails and it was difficult to tell where each ended or began, the inhabitants of Gunge squirm together as one.

Those weird ex-humans may not need sustenance to survive, but they still hunt for that which they are addicted. One and all, they are addicts. Their home in the hills is far from their prey, and they rarely hunt, but the act of it makes them a hated bunch. Their nearest prey lives a great distance from their home; they live in the cities. All who are aware of the beings that dwell in Gunge view them as monsters, and when their craving overcomes them, they are well and truly monsters.

Depending on how bizarre each creature's form has become, it can take them over a week of traveling along the grasslands at the edge of the mountains to reach the nearest village to Gunge. It is little more than a tiny hamlet and a poor hunting ground. All of the urban regions of Xin lay along the far-inland Ru River, with the richest hunting grounds in the south. However, the heavily populated capital region of Ruburge and its surrounding area are three times the distance from Gunge, and the beasts' desires are overwhelming. There are also lands to the north with prey, but treacherous mountains protect that region with a vast border of harsh terrain.

No leader reigns in Gunge. There is no hierarchy or caste system, no laws, no government, no religion. The beasts live by a new instinct, and they follow the urges of their addiction. With the physical needs of their formerly human bodies no longer a necessity, they spend idle time anticipating the next rise of their craving. There is no schedule to their desire, and when it rears its ugly head, the monsters do the same.

They rarely speak, but over the years, a single phrase became a code for their need to hunt. When an individual was coaxed by the unnatural hunger within it to leave the group, it always informed the others with the same two words, and the craving never struck more than one at a time.

Deep inside a creature who called itself Ronging, the desire sparked, and it spoke to its kin.

"I want."★

Chapter 4 – Olona, Part One

Within the township of Tuilii la Ru, one block of warehouses served as the training facilities for the organic mechanics. Olona was an apprentice, but she was acutely aware that she had already surpassed her teachers. She felt like her masters were holding her back, though she would never voice those thoughts, at least not until the arduous process of training was eventually completed.

Olona wanted to be a healer. She considered the Demifae practices to be quackery, and that mystics dabbled in things that ought not to be dabbled.

Meanwhile, here I am, she thought, *hacking apart a corpse on the orders of a master who's barely scratched the surface of the subtleties of physiological manipulation.*

Tuilii la Ru was the northernmost suburb of the grand metropolis that made up the capital city of Ruburge. In the heart of the city, life was exuberant and boisterous, but the northern region felt too old-fashioned to Olona. There were very few activities for youths outside the city limits, but the only organic mechanic apprenticeship facility was in Tuilii la Ru.

The technologies and practices of the organic mechanics were originally created by biological architects of the Oselian Empire. They developed skills in manufacturing replacement body parts and prosthetics that were unlike anything developed in all of the history of humanity's advanced achievements.

Early in Olona's childhood, she learned about the techno-healers, and a healthy obsession with their practices began to grow in her. Long before she was old enough to submit herself for evaluation as an apprentice candidate in the program, she was already practicing the old art. Any injured or dead creature that young Olona came across in the city streets, or found floating in the shallows along the banks of the mighty river were subjects of her early experimentations, and Olona was talented.

Her first major success was a dog that had lost one of its eyes. Olona was 10 years old at the time. The beast was just a mutt who lived on the street, and its injury was from long before Olona began to interact with it. After several months of feeding the dog, she managed to train it to eat out of her hands. During that time, she collected all the required parts and fashioned the crude optical replacement. She built it at her parents' kitchen table.

When it was finished, she found the dog and sat on the curb to feed it a meal. Olona patted its head several times while it was eating, then she slipped the replacement eyeball into her hand and brushed it over the dog's eyebrow. Little Olona stood up and stepped back, in case the dog reacted with aggression, but her design on the old Oselian technology was flawless. Even though the device was rudimentary, it entered the dog's orbital socket, and the animal did not flinch or yelp in pain. It simply stopped chewing, blinked *both* its eyes, and looked around in surprise. Olona approached it with a handful of food, and the mutt happily continued to eat.

Over the next several years, she managed to repair many damaged animals. A frog's broken leg was mended. Two cats that had clawed each other to pieces were also healed with her technological creations. She even fixed a fellow child's broken finger without requiring a splint.

At 14, Olona was accepted as an apprentice. Her parents were never thrilled by her fascination with organic mechanics, but they allowed their child to leave home and stay with the other apprentices to follow her dream.

However, the years of training dragged for Olona in frustrating monotony. By 17, she was already more skilled than her masters. Olona was adept at repairing or replacing almost any guild-approved part of the human body. She was also involved in an advanced research project that focused on the blood corruption disease.

There was a growing number of organic mechanics in the Tuilii la Ru region, but she was one of the very few women among them, and Olona often felt awkward around the men. Wasting her time on any of them held no interest for her; she would have liked friendship, but she hated the way the men treated her as inferior for being a woman.

One of Olona's daily responsibilities included practice on cadavers, but those experiments felt like a waste of time to her. She did not understand why the apprentices needed to keep practicing procedures on corpses when they were already performing the same techniques on living patients.

Olona knew that she could not take the additional three years of training that was required for acceptance into the guild, and she was already preparing to abandon her apprenticeship. She knew that she would need to, eventually. Olona did not have a formulated plan, but she had begun to make preparations to leave. Her skills were already to the level that she could have gone out into the world and developed new healing technologies for people.

But that's just not how we OMs do things, she thought in frustration.

There were no organic mechanic centers anywhere else in the city. Their practices were not accepted by the masses, not like those of the Demifae.

Why people trust the esoteric arts over tried and true technology, I just do not know.

There was a major Demifae neighborhood in Ruville that was called the Cauldron, and they dealt with a majority of the injured and infirmed.

They can keep their spells, Olona thought.

Many of her days were spent in similar frustrations.

She was already fulfilling most of the orders that her direct superiors received, and her evenings were kept busy building intricate replacement body parts for the few injured folks of the river lands who preferred metal to magic.

Olona's final day in the apprenticeship program arrived when she was not expecting it. She awoke that morning as if it was any other morning, and after she donned her robes and apron, she headed outside and down toward the warehouse workshop.

A trio of masters met her in the street.

"It has come to our attention," one of them barked before Olona could even greet them, "that you have performed sacred corruption upon yourself."

"You are guilty," the second declared, "and your punishment will be severe."

"Come with us now," commanded the third, "and face our wrath with the dignity of..." before he could finish, Olona's quick mind considered several variables, and she interrupted him.

"Fuck that!" she replied in a squeakier voice than she intended, and she launched herself away from the three masters.

They were shocked.

In an instant, Olona was down the street and around the corner from them. She heard their screams of "traitor" and "villain" and "freak" fading behind her.

Before the end of her second year, Olona began to regularly break one of the cardinal rules of her training, in secret. She enhanced parts of herself that did not *need* healing. There were a few organic mechanics whose past injuries had been healed with their own living machines that now dwelt inside of them, but the practice of self-enhancement was strictly forbidden. They called it *sacred corruption*. Olona did not do it as a form of rebellion, and she knew it would get her expelled from the order, but she thought it was a peculiar prohibition and one that she could not abide.

Her first act of sacred corruption, although she did not think of her enhancements in those terms, happened late one night after fixing an older man's injured leg. When she was complete with the repair, she tested his limb and realized that it was much stronger than before her treatment. Once alone, Olona repeated the process on both of her own legs. It gained her the ability to run as fast as a horse.

During the nights, she tested the mechanics that she gave herself. She was always cautious, but she was also aware that what she was doing would likely lead to serious consequences. Olona managed to give herself more enhancements than she expected before being caught, and several of them provided her with significant advantages over those who now pursued her.

She knew that it was only a matter of time before someone found out what she was doing. She was also aware that she was already outperforming her teachers and ready to leave them behind. Olona was not arrogant, but her success bolstered her confidence.

While in her apprenticeship, everything she needed for her practice was right at her fingertips. Each component that was required for creating the machines used to heal people was stored in a well-stocked organic mechanic warehouse. Over her few years in the city, Olona built connections with a few shady people who she hoped would be able to provide her with the gear that she would now need to acquire elsewhere, since the masters had found out about her internal machinery.

"Fuck those old reptiles," she said between breaths, as she raced into her home to grab the escape bag she kept hidden in the front hall closet. The strap was slung on her shoulder and she was out the door again in a matter of seconds.

Olona was sick of her apprenticeship, sick of her talents going unrecognized, sick of her small-minded masters, sick of barely making a difference when people everywhere were suffering, and most of all Olona was sick of being inhibited by those who were in control.

Her parents still lived in their home to the south of the greater Ruburge area, in the river village of Mellini. Olona suspected that her boredom in that quiet little backwater may have contributed to her creativity, and she did not intend on returning to Mellini anytime soon.

The urban sprawl of Ruburge stretched out from its center and merged with the three suburbs that surrounded it. Olona ran with unnatural speed down quiet streets through one neighborhood after another, until she was at the edge of the Ruburge city limits. She did not want to draw attention to herself and slowed her pace when she reached an area where more people were present.

There was a hostel that she regularly passed on her numerous trips into the city for the masters, and although the sign read NO VACANCIES, Olona stopped there first.

"I know you're full up," she said to the man behind the counter, "so can you recommend another cheap spot, maybe in the Ruville region?"

"Corner of 58th and Mantol streets, a place called Riverbends," the man replied without looking up at Olona.

Outside on the street again, she checked the signs. They indicated that she was at the intersection of Tankarl and 17th avenues. The roads that were labeled with the designation of *street* rather than *avenue* were clear across the city, and that was just where Olona wanted to go.

She could have arrived in the region of Riverbends in a matter of minutes if she was using her enhancements, but she walked at the same pace as the other pedestrians. It took Olona almost an hour to reach Ruville, and before she located the hostel that the man recommended, she decided to stop at a pub for a drink and a smoke and maybe even some food.

"The Goat's Maw?" she read from the sign in a curious voice. The entrance's handle was a ram's horn nailed to the door. Olona pulled it open.

Above the bar straight ahead of her was a taxidermy goat head with its mouth wide open. The tavern was crowded, with many folks enjoying a late breakfast or an early lunch.

Olona approached an empty stool, planted herself in it, and she lit a joint.

She took a puff as a barmaid asked, "Whot'll it be, luv? Ooh, don't that just smell lovely!" she commented.

Olona smiled and nodded. "I'd be very pleased with a half-pint of bitters, and that crispy bacon over there," she added, pointing at another customer's plate, "looks mighty good. I'd take a hardboiled egg and a few strips of that."

Outside the Goat's Maw, a shrill bell started to ring✪

Chapter 5 – Sumi & Harakin, Part Two

Sumi and Harakin sat up in the darkness.
The Voice was speaking.
"Wake up, twins. It's time."
The two young women waited, but the Voice said no more.
"Get dressed," whispered Sumi.
"Training drills?" Harakin asked.
Sumi shrugged.
They both pulled on their nighttime mission gear, as the door to their dormitory opened.
The man whom they referred to as the Voice entered, but he stopped in the doorframe and did not approach them.
Sumi and Harakin kept their eyes down out of habit.
"This is your location," the Voice stated, and he held up a photograph toward Sumi.

It was a castle.

He raised a second image. "And this is your primary target," the Voice added.

The picture was of an elderly man with a gray mustache and thinning hair. He was wearing a band of gold around his head set with a single gem. It may have been a simplistic design, but there was no mistaking that it was a crown.

"He will have guards," the Voice continued. "There will be counselors and advisers, and after your primary target, your orders are to eliminate as many others from his entourage as you can." He then added, "You will be going alone."

Sumi and Harakin were surprised by his words. This was the first time they were being sent on a mission without the escort of a military strike team. Sumi was part of covert attacks from time to time, but Harakin's experience outside the compound was limited to a single three-day mission along the perimeter of the Infinite Waste.

"Twin One," the Voice said to Sumi, "you will bring Twin Two through your doorway, and the pair of you will enter this location via the basement." He held up the castle image again. "The cellars and dungeons are a maze of old military tunnels. They are not difficult to navigate, and the residents rarely go below; there should be few to no enemies in the lower chambers. That is where you will begin."

The Voice held up the picture of the old man again. "Sweep through the palace, first to the throne room, and if the target is not found, proceed to the royal bed chambers. Twin Two, you are our blade in the dark," he informed Harakin. "The target and the target's associates must be eliminated. You are expected to leave many, *many* bodies in your wake."

Sumi and Harakin looked at each other.

"Twin One," the Voice said again to Sumi, "open a doorway in the basement of the castle. Focus on the image," he commanded. "Its basement exists, so find it in your mind. Then open your door."

Sumi was surprised by this information. She only ever teleported by her line of sight, and only by herself. Appearing in an unknown location seemed impossible, never mind appearing in the basement of a photograph, *and* bringing someone with her. The very idea sounded ridiculous. Sumi looked at Harakin again, turned back to the Voice, and hesitantly asked, "Confirming orders, sir, we're going away from the base?"

"Affirmative," he answered, "this mission is offsite. Now, engage, Twin One. Open a door to the cellars of this castle." He held up the image again.

"Confirming orders, sir," Sumi repeated, "I'm supposed to take Harakin through my doorway with me?"

"Affirmative," the Voice said again. "Engage."

Sumi stared at the photograph of the castle. Very little was revealed in the grainy picture, but in her mind she began to feel like she could almost see more of the structure. The rest of it seemed to come to her and she furrowed her brow in concentration. She looked over at Harakin with uncertainty and they clasped hands.

The two of them stepped through Sumi's doorway in reality, and they appeared in a dark basement of rough-hewn stone. Several torches burned along one wall. The space was cluttered, and there were no people.

"I didn't know I could do that," Sumi said in a voice of awe.

"Where are we?" Harakin whispered.

Sumi looked unsure. "I don't know, that picture, I guess." She brought her palm to one of the rough rock walls.

"Let's get this over with," Harakin said.

Sumi felt distracted. Her mind was racing with more thoughts than she was used to thinking. The horrible existence at the compound kept Sumi's creativity and imagination suppressed, and things she had never thought before now swirled in her brain.

Harakin was focused. She absorbed the faint light from the torches, and a pair of blades appeared in the air. They hovered in front of her, slowly spinning, and they moved with Harakin as she started walking forward through the narrow hallways of the cellar.

Sumi followed, and around a few corners, they came to a flight of stairs. At the top, they found a massive steel door. It would not budge.

"Wait," Sumi said, and she put her hand on Harakin's arm, "I can..." but she paused.

"What is it?" Harakin asked her.

Sumi closed her eyes. "I can feel the space on the other side of the door."

"How do we know there aren't people there?"

"There might be," Sumi said matter of factly, "and if there are, they are all targets. I can't feel if anyone's there, but I *can* feel the other side of the door."

Harakin was confused. "How is that possible?" she asked. "And how did you bring me through your doorway? And how did you open a door in someplace you've never been and couldn't see? What else can you do?"

Sumi did not reply.

Noises on the other side of the steel impediment interrupted their discussion.

"Targets acquired," Harakin whispered.

Sumi took Harakin's hand, and they stepped through Sumi's doorway into the next room. There were more people than they expected, but they neither paused nor hesitated.

Harakin's two hovering blades launched forward through the air and stabbed into a pair of startled-looking men of the king's court. More glowing weapons materialized around Harakin that slashed and spun and hacked into flesh, and a moment later, she and Sumi were the only living people in the room.

Seven corpses lay sprawled on the polished marble floor of the hall.

Sumi and Harakin examined each of them.

"These are all secondary targets."

"Where's the throne room?" asked Harakin.

"I can..." Sumi began again.

Harakin waited. "What?" she asked. "You can what?"

Sumi closed her eyes. "I can feel it."

She reached out for Harakin's hand, and they stepped through another one of her doorways that led beyond reality. They appeared in the huge throne room. It was dark and silent, and the royal chairs sat empty at the other end of it.

"No one's in here," Harakin whispered.

"Look," Sumi said, and she pointed, "behind the thrones, that door opens to a set of stairs."

Torches around the room suddenly flared to life, illuminating the hall in bright light, as a woman descended the stairs and entered the throne room.

She froze, but then she scowled at the two intruders and barked at them, "Who dares enter the hall of the king?! I am queen of the river realm, and I demand…" but her voice was cut off, along with her head.

Harakin was on the woman in a flash, and her blades sliced through the queen's neck as easily as lopping off the flower of a dandelion.

Her crowned head hit the floor with a clank and a wet flub noise. A fountain of blood erupted from her body.

Sumi began to say, "Secondary target elimin…" but she too was interrupted.

A voice behind the headless queen screamed, as the woman's body slumped to a pile on the floor. Three youths stood frozen on the lowest steps. They were too shocked to move.

The scream drew the attention of unseen guards who came rushing into the throne room, and the king himself pushed passed his children. He stopped dead in his tracks, and he wailed at the sight of his wife's corpse.

Sumi and Harakin then did what they were trained to do. Even though Harakin was closer to their primary target, she turned to deal with the guards, and Sumi traded places with her.

The old man positioned himself between his children and Sumi's oncoming assault. He drew his mighty sword and roared at her.

Sumi stepped through one of her doorways, and she took the king's torso with her, but she left his arm and his weapon in the throne room.

The sword clanged to the floor, still clutched in the king's hand, but his legs did not fall. They stood rigid like a horrible statue, and with nothing to contain what innards remained, the king's intestines sloughed from atop his hips down onto his sword.

His three children were barely given an instant to shriek or cry at seeing their parents murdered.

Sumi stepped up to them, and she walked through one of her doorways with the two elder princelings' heads.

The young princess stared at the carnage in terror and tears ran down her face. Her brothers' decapitated bodies fell beside the remains of her parents.

Then Sumi passed through another one of her doors, and the entire child was gone. Sumi turned from the corpses of the royal family, to see Harakin slaughtering an entire squadron of soldiers.

Bodies squirmed on the floor all around her, as the life within them poured from the grievous wounds caused by her conjured weapons. The blades of light surrounded Harakin, and her vicious weapons impaled and gouged and cut through the men's armor, cleaving deep into their flesh. She cut off hands and arms and heads, but the anguished cries of the dying were temporary, and Harakin silenced them.

Blades flashed into existence with the speed of her thoughts, and the humans who dared to challenge her were no match. She ducked below a soldier's sword swipe, and she chopped through both of his legs. As he fell, Harakin rose like a monstrous surgeon surrounded by the amputated limbs of her enemies.

Sumi's feelings of success were then dashed right before her eyes.

The legless soldier was writhing on the floor at Harakin's feet, but before his life was sapped, he managed to grab a fallen spear and thrust it up at her.

To Sumi's horror, the weapon's tip sliced deep into Harakin's neck, and her blood spurted once before she slammed her hands over her throat.

Harakin fell to her knees.

"No!" screamed Sumi. She rushed through one of her mystical doorways to Harakin. Sumi reached out to take her hand, so they could escape with her power, but another soldier was charging at Harakin, and he crashed into Sumi. She fell, sprawling to the tiled throne room floor.

Another guard was on her, and he swung his club down. Sumi threw up her arm in a defensive move, and his blow collided with it. She felt the two bones in her forearm snap, and she cried out in pain. Sumi clutched her damaged limb with her opposite hand, and someone grabbed her from behind. They yanked her away from Harakin and threw her across the hard stone floor.

Sumi's eyes shot to Harakin.

Her injured companion gasped the word, "Go!" with her face full of pleading. Harakin released one hand from the terrible wound that was pouring blood from her neck, and she reached above her head. "*Go!*" she managed a second time.

Sumi knew what was happening.

In the air above Harakin, she manifested a storm of blades. She conjured so many in an instant that they pushed against the walls of the chamber, and the very stone of the castle itself began to buckle. Harakin gritted her teeth and made eye contact with Sumi one last time, as the hand Harakin held aloft formed a fist.

Sumi activated her unique ability as a life-saving reflex, and she disappeared through one of her doorways, as Harakin's countless daggers of energetic lightforce came crashing down on the throne room floor.

All within were slain, and the royal structure itself began to collapse.

Sumi suddenly found herself standing alone in the dark silence of the dormitory.

The Voice crackled to life. "Mission accomplished?" it asked. Then the Voice added in a tone of surprise, "Where is Twin Two?

The pain in Sumi's broken arm was causing her head to spin, and she collapsed to the floor.

When she came to, she was strapped down to a gurney and several medics were standing over her.

"My arm," she moaned.

"The bones have already been set," one of them stated, "and the arm is bound with a splint. It will take time to heal."

Sumi winced.

Then the Voice repeated itself. "Where is Twin Two?"

Sumi's eyes went wide with realization, and tears streamed down her cheeks; she did not possess the will to stop them.

"They killed her," she bawled.

"Was the mission a success?" the Voice asked.

"She's dead!" Sumi cried.

"Was the mission successful?!" the Voice yelled.

"Yes," Sumi whimpered, "mission complete."

The Voice went silent.

"You're nearly patched up," said one of the medics. "I'll bring you to your quarters."

He released the straps, helped Sumi into a wheelchair, and rolled her out of the room. However, when he turned her down the hallway that led away from the dormitory, Sumi started to panic.

"No, wait!" she pleaded. "Why?! Not the black cell!"

The fear within her diminished Sumi to the cowering child who was first abducted and brought to the compound. She writhed in the wheelchair but was powerless to stop the guard from opening the putrid chamber and pushing the chair into it. He closed the door behind her.

The sobs that wracked Sumi's body managed to dredge up the little girl who still lived deep inside of her. The despair in the crawling darkness of the cell overwhelmed her, and Sumi's mind tumbled into delirium★

Chapter 6 – Tisa & the Witch, Part Two

In the hut beside Liovia's hollow, Tisa awoke with a start. She sat bolt upright and listened. The forest was silent. She did not know what she heard, but something had made a brief horrible noise.

Tisa pulled on a fresh shirt and her trousers, and she headed outside. Not a sound came from anything around her. Even the breeze seemed to have vanished.

"Liovia?" Tisa called out to the witch. "Did you hear something?" Tisa was half-asleep, and she yawned and stretched. There was no reply, and she stuck her head in the muddy hole beneath the tree, but the witch was not inside.

"Liovia!" Tisa called, but in the silence of the forest, she restrained her voice from being too loud.

Again, she received no answer. Tisa thought she was going to need to search the nearby woods, but the witch was just on the other side of her tree.

She was in a state that Tisa had never witnessed.

Liovia was in a seated position, but she was floating above the ground. Her wings were spread wide, although they did not seem to have anything to do with her levitation. The witch was in a trance, and her hair was waving in all directions as if she was underwater. There was still no breeze, yet her locks flowed.

"Liovia?" Tisa whispered. She stepped closer to the witch, and the woman spoke in syllables that Tisa could not decipher.

"Imalu akaa mu sooli om cala."

"I don't know what that means," Tisa replied when the witch stopped speaking.

Liovia then repeated herself with only a slight variation. "Imalu akaa mu sooli om alau."

"What are you saying?"

Tisa was used to the witch's tendency to talk about the future as if it were happening in the moment, but she never heard her speak in another language, and the hovering was new.

"Ommu sha triilii ah oh um."

Tisa was at a loss. "I don't know what I'm supposed to do," she said, more to herself than the witch.

"Mistal ooi," Liovia concluded. Her seated position lowered and returned to the earth. She opened her eyes, and the witch told Tisa, "We must hurry."

"What was all that? I've never seen you do that, and hurry where? Liovia!"

The witch stood, turned, and headed south along the river. "It was a protective premonition," she said as Tisa followed. "I don't often need to look into my own future, because it is always clear to me. Only in moments that lack clarity, does it necessitate me tapping into a deeper region of my sight," she explained.

Then the witch declared, "We need to find the girl. We need to find the boy. A monster is approaching. It is not far."

Tisa paused. "Is that what you were saying? What boy and what girl?"

"The four of us need to leave now," the witch replied.

"Four?" Tisa asked.

Liovia stopped, stared at Tisa, and she said, "Four of us, four days, we need supplies. We leave as soon as I return."

Tisa was confused. "You want me to pack?"

The witch left her standing among the trees.

"Alright," Tisa said to herself, "four days' worth of supplies for four people." She did not know what the witch knew, but she did know to take the witch's words seriously, even when they did not make much sense.

Less than an hour later, Liovia returned with two young teenagers. The boy and the girl looked confused and afraid.

Tisa approached them the way she did on the rare occasion when someone came seeking knowledge of their future from the witch. "Welcome to the hollow," she said in a bright voice. Only adults ever came to visit the witch, and the youths were the youngest people Tisa had seen in years. "Do you two need some advice?" she asked.

"We need to leave," Liovia stated.

"It's after us," the girl said.

"I don't want it to get us," added the boy.

Tisa furrowed her brow. "What is going on?!"

"An eater of souls is coming."

Tisa's blood went cold. "I didn't think that was what you meant. Coming here? There hasn't been one in years!"

"It wants us," Liovia replied, "or the children."

"Let's go then," Tisa said, unsure where they were headed.

As the witch led them away, Tisa asked her, "How did you convince the children to come with you? Do their parents know?"

"Their parents' knowledge is inconsequential," Liovia replied. "I *showed* the children, let them see their future if they chose not to follow me."

"What do you mean? I thought you just informed people of their future. You can actually show them?"

Liovia sighed and took a deep breath. "I learned in the beginning that showing the future always negated it for the viewer. However, if I *tell* vague possibilities about a future, it remains possible."

Tisa was amazed at all she was learning that day about the woman with whom she had spent so much of her life. The witch was always a mystery, but this revelation was astounding to Tisa; Liovia was so much more than a fortuneteller.

"How are we going to keep the monster from finding us?" Tisa asked.

"It will search the village for a matter of hours," Liovia replied, "and then it will travel south until it finds what it seeks."

"So, we only have to stay away until it's gone?"

"It will leave the village unsatisfied."

"Good," Tisa replied, "well, then, lead the way, I guess."

The four began to head into the thicker forest that grew on the foothills of the northern mountains, and through that rugged terrain, they hiked for three long days.

On their third evening, the witch informed Tisa and the two youths, "It has begun to travel south. We must remain another day, and then we can return."

They ceased their seemingly aimless hiking and rested for the entire following day. On the fifth morning, the group of four made their way out of the forest and back down to Kestapoli, but the villagers were in an uproar before they arrived.

Three people were dead✪

Chapter 7 – Ronging

Leaving the realm of monsters, Ronging set out to sate his unworldly desire. The expansive grasslands were easy enough to cross, but the distance took time. Over the recent decades, the inhabitants of Gunge learned that because of the witch, the nearest human village of Kestapoli was a poor hunting ground. She always knew when one of them was on the hunt, and she would be gone before they arrived.

She was the prey that the monsters craved, she and those like her, few though they were.

Ronging's eldritch senses honed in on the witch, and despite the potential failure, his desire urged him to head toward the nearest village. His journey to the fertile hunting grounds that surrounded Ruburge would have taken so much longer than his trip to Kestapoli, and Ronging was impatient to satisfy his craving. However, if the witch escaped and he could not find prey in the village, his journey south along the snaking Ru River would end up being much longer. The next nearest town of Galopis was several days further journey to the south, and like Kestapoli, it was also a small community. There was a chance that Ronging would find no prey to hunt.

Like all the monstrous inhabitants of Gunge, Ronging wore no clothes on his bizarre and twisted form. He lumbered with a strange canter that was unique to him. Each of the creatures moved differently. Many slithered, some crawled, but Ronging possessed a form that allowed him a semblance of walking. His body was humanoid in its original construction, but over his years of addiction, since first becoming a Messiah, he was very changed.

Ronging was born a human child to human parents. At the age of 19, he consumed the photonova gland that enhanced him to a Messiah. While on his first hunting mission, Ronging achieved the goal set before him, and he found himself in possession of a photonova gland from the Shift he was sent to murder. Instead of returning to the Messiah Tower with it, he swallowed the crystal.

To his dismay, Ronging did not get another boost to his strength as he expected. Instead, pain struck his entire being, as a third arm manifested from his stomach. It reached forward fully formed, but that was only the beginning. A secondary mouth opened in his neck and a massive fleshy protuberance bulged out from his upper back. One of his feet sprouted multiple extra toes, and three new testicles bulged in their very own oversized scrotum that hung down behind the one he possessed at birth.

Ronging hobbled with bowlegged steps through the Teshon City streets back to the temple. He was full of fear, yet uncertain what else he could do.

His eldest sister dwelled at the Tower. She was not only a role model for him, but she was also a high-ranking and decorated Messiah officer. Her mutated younger brother rushed into her private chambers.

As he slammed the door behind him, understanding immediately sank in for his sister, and she snapped at him, *"What the fuck is wrong with you?!"*

"I didn't know!" Ronging said in a strange dual voice. His new mouth spoke with a whiny timber that grated in an off-key pitch against the voice that came out of his natural mouth.

"How the fuck," his sister barked, "did you not know?! No Messiahs consume a second photonova gland! This is your own fault, and before you ask, there's nothing, absolutely nothing that can be done about it." She stood behind her desk and declared, "Ronging, my brother, you are hereby exiled from Teshon City and all its surrounding regions."

"But..." he began to protest.

"Far to the south," she yelled, "you will find refuge among others of your..." she paused and sneered at her younger brother with revulsion, "your own kind. Follow the coastline beyond Hazel Cove. The banishment you face is permanent. Do not return. Do not seek an audience with the Messiahs of this city." She glared at him. "And as far as family is concerned, you are disowned. You disgust me, little brother. I will never again speak your name. Now go. Get out. Make your way south alone and abandoned." She scowled and pointed at the door behind him.

Tears were streaming down Ronging's cheeks.

"Sister," he began, but she shouted over him.

"You are no kin of mine! Be gone, or face worst punishments!" As a final gesture, which might have been construed as kindness, his sister threw her own cloak at him to hide his hideous form.

Ronging fled Teshon City with nothing more than the clothes on his back, none of which fit his now-twisted body, and the garment from his sister. At the time, he did not know what lay beyond the vast mountain range to the south of the fishing villages that dotted the coast.

Ronging traveled in the rough land off the Great Southtrack to keep his weird new form hidden from view, and on his sixth day, he reached the high cliffs that rose above the ocean beyond the last little seaside hamlet of Hazel Cove.

Into that mountainous wilderness, alone and in misery, Ronging made his way south. He journeyed for many days before he realized that he had not eaten during the entire time. With his human form forever gone, hunger no longer plagued him. His travel was slow, and a full three months after beginning his journey, Ronging arrived at a rise that provided him his first view of the plains of Xin. That night, he found the monsterdom of Gunge.

More than three decades had passed since those early days of his mutation, and his form grew more twisted each time his addiction required that he hunt. Ronging's third photonova gland caused him to grow an extra leg from his right hip. It slowed his already bowlegged walk, but he was still able to move in an upright manner. He also developed an extra set of eyes, but both grew on his right cheek and neither of them could see very well. His next photonova gland produced yet a third leg on his right side. It made his walk even stranger, with his lone left leg swinging out to the side with each lurching step. He also developed another penis that sprouted from his low back, but neither of his penises functioned.

All human urges diminished and eventually disappeared, replaced by only the addiction. Hunger and thirst, even breathing were no longer part of Ronging's existence, and bodily exhaustion did not affect those who were mutated. The next photonova gland would be his fifth.

On the hunt again to satisfy the only craving that reared its head, Ronging made his way along the edge of the forested mountains of northern Xin. He moved with his awkward shamble, slow but with the determination that came with his single-mindedness.

Six tedious days Ronging lumbered, his craving ever-increasing, until he eventually reached the village. His unearthly senses led him first to the witch's muddy home and the little shack that stood beside it, but there was no one there with a photonova gland. He drew close to Kestapoli, but he stayed hidden in the wooded area to the north for the remainder of the daylight hours.

The sun slowly set and night fell.

Ronging slunk out of the trees and into the quiet village. He allowed his craving to lead him toward the prey that he sought; he could sense them.

The anguished cries of a woman broke the stillness and drew Ronging's attention, but then he was aware of other things that were much more delicious to him. Outside of a large building, Ronging paused and listened to her wailing voice while savoring the photonova glands that he could detect.

"Our children have been out there for days!"

Another voice spoke quieter, but Ronging was still able to make out the words.

"There's nothing more we can do tonight."

"Don't tell me it's hopeless!" the first voice cried. "Don't tell *us* it's hopeless!"

Ronging peered through a window. Two women were embracing, and both were in tears. A third who was much older was with them, and a pair of ineffectual men stood off to one side, whispering to each other.

The motherly woman tried to comfort the distraught woman. "The sun has set, child, we will go ba…"

"Why is that an excuse to stop looking for my baby?" the woman snapped. She broke down in sobs that shook her body, and the other young woman held her.

"Both of us have missing children," she said. "We are doing everything we can. I know that we have no comfort now, but we will get them back. Our children are…"

Ronging could wait no longer, and he smashed through the wall of the building, shocking those who were inside. He grabbed the two men with his multiple arms, and his enhanced strength made them putty in his hands. Both of them screamed in terror, as the monster pulled their heads toward his mouths and breathed in their aromas. Although both men possessed a lingering scent of what he craved, neither was his prey.

He roared, pushed them away, and grabbed all three women at once. Ronging sniffed each, but again, he was denied his desire. There were no photonova glands within anyone present.

Both of the men pounced on Ronging from behind, and a rage boiled up in him equaled only by his addiction. To the horror of them all, Ronging grabbed one of the men and ripped off his arm. He lashed out at the four others, pummeling them with the limb until no one was moving, and he again exited through the hole he made in the wall.

Ronging's senses told him that the ones whom he could detect were now far from Kestapoli, and in fury he departed. However, just outside of town, he came upon a pair of villagers. His craving crazed him, and he grabbed them with his multiple hands and raised them above his head. He slammed the two people down to the path, raising them and smashing them against the hard-packed earth over and over. He left their bodies as little more than bloody pulp and shards of bone.

Ronging could be heard shrieking and bellowing long after he was out of sight. He stomped through the next five days and nights, as his addiction evolved into a searing pain, a hot poker jabbing into his soul. The gnawing desire within him continued to ache as the sun rose over his twisted form, but on the sixth morning, there was still a full day's journey ahead, and on he lumbered. At sundown, he finally arrived at the next riverside town.

However, the inhabitants of Kestapoli sent word downriver, warning of the approaching monster, and the people of Galopis were prepared in advance to protect themselves. Their lookouts saw Ronging when he was still at a distance, and their defensive measures were in place as he drew close. Galopis was larger than

Kestapoli, and a small battalion of the king's guards from Ruburge garrisoned it. They were well-trained.

Being a former Messiah made Ronging invulnerable to most assaults, but the villagers protected their land with a perpetual barrage of targeted catapult fire that pummeled him through the night. Eventually, the infuriated monster was driven around the edge of town and forced out into the sprawling grasslands.

Ronging stormed away from Galopis. He knew that what his addiction required would be found in the grand metropolis and surrounding region of greater Ruburge farther to the south, but his entire being was burning with need. It would be a further four days of travel before he reached the outskirts of the city, and the need brought on by his addiction would only continue to scorch his soul until he found what he hunted.

Someone in Ruburge was going to die★

Chapter 8 – Olona, Part Two

A man entered the Goat's Maw with a large bell in his hand. *"Oi, ye lot!"* he called out over the hubbub of the tavern.

Olona looked in his direction.

"Oi! 'Ear ye, 'ear ye!" the man said with a thick accent. "Dis is a call out for any 'ealers! To de far nort' of our lands, de village of Kestapoli done suffered an 'orrific attack. Some of dem residents be needing care."

Olona perked up, took another puff from her joint, and handed it to the barmaid. She then headed toward the man.

"I can help," Olona declared to him.

He gave her a doubtful look-over. "Ain't ye a bit young?"

"I've been trained in healing," she replied. She did not mention what type of healing she did, in case the man was adverse to organic mechanics.

Olona ended up being the only one in the pub interested or willing to make the river journey north.

The man headed on to another bar, as Olona ate her breakfast. She then headed back to the part of the city where her former masters were looking for her, and she purchased a ticket for the northbound ferry from Tuilii la Ru. The local rivercraft was the

fastest way north, but when she arrived at the dock, there was a 30-minute wait before the next departure.

Olona raced back to the house where she had lived for three years as an apprentice, to collect a few more of her things that were not part of her emergency bag. Several people in the street were very surprised to see the young woman go past them faster than a normal human, but she was long gone before any of them could react.

She turned onto the boulevard with her address, and sure enough, several masters were out front. They were talking together and pointing at her front door, and they looked angry.

"Dammit," she growled.

Olona turned and flew back through the city at a dizzying speed. When she was near the docks again, she found a quiet alley and zipped into it. If anyone was after her because of seeing her use her enhancements, she knew that she could rush off again. When she was sure that the coast was clear, Olona stepped out of the alleyway and walked the last few blocks at a normal pace. She walked up to the captain of the ferry and handed him her ticket with a smile.

Two hours later, Olona was halfway to Kestapoli, and she arrived at the town of Galopis; the citizens were on high alert. There were only 10 minutes between her arrival and the departure of the connecting ferry that was going to take her on the second leg of the journey.

Olona spent the brief time questioning the locals who were on the wharf. They confirmed for Olona that a monster had attacked the town of Kestapoli at sunset the evening before, and Galopis was preparing itself to make a defensive stand against the creature. The people informed Olona that it would still be a matter of days before the thing would make it to Galopis, but they needed to be diligent if they hoped to protect themselves.

The next river ship departed with Olona and a few others who were headed the rest of the way north. Kestapoli came into view just under two hours later. When they arrived, Olona immediately made herself known, and she was directed to the makeshift infirmary that was set up for the wounded villagers.

The victims who had survived the monster's attack were in a bad state. One woman was heavily bandaged. She was hunched over, seated on a gurney, and groaning in pain. An older woman was stretched out in a coma. There was a nasty gash on her cheek that was bandaged, but blood still seeped from it. In one corner, another woman was whimpering to herself and would not respond to anyone. Strapped down to a bed was a man; he was twitching. A bandage patch was over one eye, and another covered his ear. Both of his arms and both of his legs were bound with splints, and his breathing came in slow wheezes.

Olona stepped up to the healer who was overseeing the injured.

"I'm an organic mechanic from Ruburge," she informed the woman. "How can I help?"

The healer gave Olona an uncertain glance, and she asked, "What are you allowed to heal?"

Olona knew that was a common question that came up for organic mechanics, even though the whole idea of limiting her ability to heal seemed preposterous. "What's wrong with her?" Olona asked, pointing at the unconscious older woman.

"Severe concussion with a deep laceration to the cheek."

Olona was not permitted under the guidelines of her order to revive someone from a concussion. "I can help with the face wound. What about the others?"

"Broken all four limbs," the healer said, pointing at the man. "Lost an eye and a lot of blood," she added. She turned to the bruised woman. "Several broken ribs on her right side, multiple lacerations, some severe." Then she pointed at the last woman. "She's been partially catatonic, won't react to anything, just keeps crying."

Olona nodded. "I can speed the healing of all the broken bones, but I don't have the equipment for his eye." Olona turned to the unresponsive woman in the corner. "What happened to her?"

The healer tutted. "Found out her kid's one of them Shifts."

"*No!*" the woman suddenly shrieked. "No, she's not! I didn't birth one of those freaks!"

"She did," the healer said to Olona.

"Nooo!" the woman howled.

The healer ignored her even though she was now responding. "Her daughter is fine. The witch took her and a boy out of here before the monster showed up."

"Kidnapped!" the woman screamed.

"She doesn't seem catatonic anymore," Olona commented. "What does she mean? And what witch?"

"The witch of the whitewater," the healer explained, "a local fortune teller. She knew the monster was coming, snatched them kids who it would have eaten, and she hid them in the forest."

Then the woman in the corner roared. "We killed her!"

"Your daughter?!" Olona asked in a shocked voice.

"No," the healer said quietly, "the witch and her helper brought the children back unharmed," she paused and looked over at the raving woman, "and they murdered the witch."

"*For saving the children?*" Olona squawked.

The formerly-catatonic woman cackled. "And we chased her little minion out into the Infinite Waste! She was the first one, years ago, the first one the witch got under her spell, the first one the witch took, and then she took my daughter!" The woman wailed.

"Glad I was apparently able to help with the catatonia, as well," Olona whispered to the healer, while she began to treat the man's broken limbs.

Outside, the sun slowly set, and Olona kept working on the four survivors late into the night. When she completed all of the permitted healing techniques, she finally headed out into the darkness.

Kestapoli was silent. Even the inn seemed unwelcoming with only a single candle burning in one window.

Olona's mind turned to the extra information she had received from the angry woman, and she looked into the Infinite Waste. Someone was lost out there, may have been lost for an entire day already. Olona did not know how she could find the witch's helper. She was tired from her whirlwind of a day but opted to continue even farther north. Olona wanted to see if she could find the so-called witch's former dwelling. She came across the witch first.

Tied to an old knotty tree was a dead woman. She was naked, and every inch of her skin was marked with strange patterning. Ropes were wrapped around her corpse many times from her ankles to her neck. The shafts of several arrows protruded from her torso and limbs, and a pile of rocks at her feet made it clear what the townsfolk did.

Tears sprang from Olona's eyes at the sight of the abused and murdered woman.

"I'm done helping these villagers," Olona said between her gritted teeth. She wiped her eyes hard.

Olona stepped around two large pieces of thick scaly material that lay beside the tree. A boulder was on top of them. She could not tell what the material was, but she did not like the look of the things. Olona lit a joint, and little clouds of smoke puffed into the air above her head as she continued upstream.

Less than an hour later, she found a hut.

"Hello," Olona called out, "is anyone there? I'm a healer from the south, Ruburge." She was hopeful that the witch's helper made it back from the Infinite Waste, but she received no reply and approached the little house.

"Hello!?" Olona knocked on the door.

Still, no one answered.

She sat down on one of the chairs outside the little dwelling.

The witch's corpse flashed into her mind, and Olona wished she could leave Xin to find a life for herself, where people were different than Xinitians.

Her exhaustion brought more tears to her eyes. The suspicious and backwater folk of Kestapoli were just as horrible as her restrictive teachers, but in their own uniquely cruel way.

Olona cried into her hands.

"*What do you want?*" barked a voice off to one side.

Olona put up her palms in a peaceful gesture, and she peered through the darkness. "I'm just a healer," she said quickly, sniffing hard to force down her tears. "I arrived from Ruburge earlier to help the injured."

"There's no injured here. Leave."

The question that Olona then asked surprised even herself. "Why are you staying in this place?" The words felt rude as they left her lips, and Olona regretted phrasing it as she did.

"That's my home."

A woman stepped out from the trees. She was thin and tall, and she looked severe.

"I mean," Olona tried to reword her thought, "why are you staying here, now that the witch is..." her voice trailed off.

"Her name was Liovia," said the woman in a tone that sounded hollow and overwhelmed by misery.

"The people of the village," Olona said, "they are horrible."

"They're my people," the woman retorted.

Olona tried to choose her next words carefully, but she was tired. She sighed. "Why don't you just leave?"

"And go where?"

"Anywhere," Olona replied, "what about down south, Ruburge, or the surrounding area?"

"Look, girl," the woman said, "I've spent most of my life in this forest, I can't go anywhere else."

"What about going," Olona paused, "erm… northerly?"

The woman looked startled.

"And my name's Olona."

"Why did you say it like that?" the woman whispered in a voice of shock.

Olona was puzzled. "Because," she replied, "it's… erm… my name?"

"No, the word *north*. Why did you say it like that? Northerly."

"I don't know. I'm really tired," Olona stated. "I think I just mispronounced it. I don't know what I'm saying. I just came up here to see if you needed help, but since you seem to be in need of nothing, I'll be on my…"

"Liovia used to repeat a line with that word," the woman interrupted. "She used to say it out of the blue, for no reason at all. *Life is northerly.* She never explained it and I always dismissed it as more of her nonsense." She fell silent.

"I'm sorry," Olona said quietly. "I'm sorry she's gone, and I'm so sorry for how it happened."

"Please, don't apologize for someone else's villainy."

Olona hesitated, then asked, "What's your name?"

The woman sighed. "Tisa," she said.

"Tisa, I'm sorry Liovia is gone."

The tough facade cracked, and Tisa broke down in tears.

Olona cautiously approached and placed her hand on Tisa's shoulder. Her crying slowly diminished after several minutes, and Olona asked in a gentle voice, "Was she your mother?"

Tisa spoke between her shuddering breaths. "She was like a mother, or maybe more like a big sister," she added. "I've lived here with her for more than half my life. I have no one else and nowhere else to go. And I don't know *why* you just said northerly," Tisa continued, shaking her head, "or what Liovia meant. There's no life up north; there are only mountains and more forest."

Olona was curious. "Did she say anything else when she said *life is northerly*, anything along with it?"

Tisa rubbed her eyes. "No, like I said, she would just say it from time to time, no rhyme or reason."

"Did she have other things she said that made no sense?"

Tisa scoffed and another tear trickled down her cheek. "Half of what she said was nonsense. I don't know if she saw the future, or if she was somehow living in a past version of herself or something. In all that time with her, I never figured it out, and she never really explained it to me."

"I wish we could just leave Xin," Olona mumbled, and she yawned. "Ugh, I'm so tired."

"Let's go inside," Tisa offered. "I'm also ready for sleep. You can rest with me here. It's safe."

"Safe?" Olona questioned. "With those townsfolk just a short hike away? It doesn't seem very safe."

"I assure you," Tisa replied, "no one can enter the witch's region without permission."

"Well," Olona replied, "I did."

"I wasn't here, so preventing you was not necessary. Through the night, we will be protected."

Tisa's words brought unexpected comfort to Olona.

"Come inside with me," Tisa urged, "and I know that you said your name, but I've already lost it. Please, tell me again."

"Olona," she said as they both entered. "How old are you?" she asked.

Tisa looked contemplative. "Birthdays were meaningless here in the forest with the absentmindedness of Liovia, but I'm fairly certain that I'm 30, or thereabouts."

"Wow, you're old," Olona replied. She slapped her hands over her mouth. "I didn't mean that," she whispered.

"Nice," said Tisa with a sarcastic smirk, "and what are you, 14?"

"I'm 17, thank you very much," Olona replied in her own snotty tone.

"Okay, kid, you're alright," Tisa's smile got a little bigger. "Here, let's get you set up on the cot, and we can get some sleep. Again, now that I'm here, no one can enter the region. You're safe."

"Thank you," Olona said.

"And thank you," Tisa replied, "for helping the injured people from my village."

Olona scoffed. "Fuck them, and fuck that town. Sorry," she added.

"No," Tisa agreed, "you're right."

"What other weird things did the witch, I mean Liovia, used to say?"

"Oh, I don't know," Tisa replied, as she gave Olona a blanket and climbed into her own bed. "She used to say all kinds of things, but I don't know if I can think of them offhand."

The two fell silent, and although they both felt awkward about the situation, Olona was soon asleep. Tisa lay awake, pondering her encounter with the girl. Eventually, she too drifted into slumber.

Tisa awoke as the sun rose. She waited for Olona to wake up as well, and when she did, Tisa told her, "I thought of another. *Don't forget to go to the coast first.* That's something Liovia used to say at ridiculous times. While cooking, *don't forget to go to the coast first.* Repairing the cottage, *don't forget to go to the coast first.* Fishing in the Ru…"

"*Don't forget to go to the coast first?*" Olona interrupted.

"Exactly," Tisa replied, "I think that's our route."

"Wait," Olona responded, "*our* route?"

"I think you're right," Tisa explained. "I thought about it for a long time last night. I think we need to leave the land of Xin. Will you come with me?"✪

Chapter 9 – Sumi

It was night when the countless hours of Sumi's torment in the black cell finally came to an end. She was released and hosed off beneath a half-moon before being sent to the empty dormitory.

Harakin's space and possessions brought fresh tears to Sumi's eyes, and she fell onto her prison mate's bed. She rolled on her back, looked at the grey ceiling, and she heard Harakin's words in her mind, *What else can you do?*

"I wish I knew more about my powers," Sumi said aloud. Then she thought, *I wish I could open a door that told me everything about them.*

The eldritch energies within her activated of their own accord, and Sumi could feel one of her doorways. It did not open at her command to step through, it just simply *was*. She did not know why it was there, but it almost seemed to be waiting for her. Sumi rubbed her eyes, sat up, and swung her legs over the side of Harakin's bed.

She stepped through her doorway into an office. It was empty.

Sumi was positioned directly in front of a filing cabinet. One of her hands was holding the handle of its second drawer. She pulled it open, and Sumi immediately saw her name.

Even though she thought that she did not know how to read, the letters and symbols revealed their meanings to her probing eyes. She pulled out the file and stared at her full name printed across the top of it. The last time she had heard it spoken aloud was thirteen years earlier, and more than half of her lifetime. Sumi barely remembered it.

"Oligana Nisumi Mong," she read aloud. It felt strange to say her old name, the name her parents gave to her, but it was as dead to her as they were.

"Sumi," she whispered, as if to reassure herself who she was.

A large sticker with red letters took up much of the folder's cover. Sumi read it aloud also.

"Preliminary findings too extreme. Experimentation canceled."

She opened the file and continued, but the words were confusing.

"One," she read, "subject possesses the ability to enter a congruent dimension that appears to exist solely for subject." Sumi paused.

"What does that mean?" she asked the empty room, and she continued.

"Two, subject can remain in congruent dimension for an indeterminate amount of time with no adverse effects. Three, subject can bring multiple other individuals through congruent dimension. Four, subject can bring individuals into congruent dimension for extended periods of time, but others are neither conscious nor aware of time spent therein."

This is really repetitive, Sumi thought, and her brow furrowed as she read more.

"Five, subject can utilize congruent dimension as viewing position. Subject possesses capacity to peer into reality from congruent dimension before stepping out of congruent dimension back into reality."

Sumi turned the page.

"Summary: Subject possesses capacity to teleport anywhere, limited only by subject's imagination and also driven by it. Subject enters a unique realm, can exist in it, and can see the real world from within. Recommendations: One, instill fear of congruent dimension in subject. Alternatively, subject should be trained to immediately step through dimensional portal, spending no time in congruent dimension. Two, limit subject's teleportation distance by training subject to only teleport by line of sight. Three, train subject to use dimensional portal to remove portions of targets for efficient elimination."

What I really want, Sumi thought, *is a door that will bring me to Harakin*, and again, she felt one of her doorways appear.

Noises outside the office startled her, and without hesitation she stepped through reality.

Sumi found herself standing in a waist-high labyrinth of overgrown hedges. The office, the filing cabinet, even the compound were gone. The file, however, was not. Sumi was still holding the folder.

The cultivated rows of plants that now surrounded her were left untended and on the verge of going wild, but they led to the ruins of a large stone structure that loomed against the sky. The moon glowed down upon the old broken stones.

Sumi was right in the middle of the scraggly maze, and surrounding the entire courtyard were trees. The wooded area also appeared to have been planted deliberately, and it stretched up to the ruins on either side, encircling the area. Its trees were overgrown but seemed more recently tended where they grew nearest to the dilapidated ruins.

It looked to Sumi like life at this fort had come to a crashing halt.

The old stone building was buckled in the middle. The majority of its two sidewalls still stood, but the center and roof were caved-in. It appeared that whatever wooden support beams used to exist must have rotted away long ago and caused the ceiling to collapse. The ruins looked ancient. Their grey stones were bleached by countless years beneath the hot sun that beat down on the lands of Xin.

Questions swirled in Sumi's brain. Where was she? Why was she there? What were these ruins? Maybe more importantly, why were her doorways now opening seemingly on their own?

Sumi decided that the trees and labyrinth would not reveal much more to her than they already did, and she began to weave through the paths. She climbed over a few sections where the maze led away from the ruins, and more questions arose in her mind.

Who planted the hedges and weeded the pathways in between? Where were the gardeners? What formerly great families used to keep these lands?

Leading up to the collapsed structure stretched a wide set of stone steps and a grand patio. When the old building fell, its crumbled masonry spread out as a jumbled mess into the space that was once clean and organized.

Sumi headed to one side of the ruins and made her way through the trees toward the front. A moment later, she came out on the sprawling terrace that led up to the fallen stones.

The devastation to the old structure appeared even worse from the front than it did from the back. She thought it looked like a terrible barrage of cannon fire pounded against the building until it was destroyed.

Sumi did not know why, but she felt a familiarity with this place. She did not recognize the ruins, but there was a nagging in her that they were something; the ruins were important.

There was no way for her to enter what remained of the structure, but Sumi walked up to where its front doors may have once stood. She looked over the stillness and tried to imagine what else could have caused the castle to fall.

Castle! Sumi thought.

The ruins became clear in her mind. It was the site of their royal assassination mission.

Sumi was shocked. In her mind, she could see the picture that the Voice showed her. This was that building, but mere hours earlier it was an immovable and imposing edifice. Now, it was no more than ruins.

Above Sumi's head, there was a flash of light, and she was even more shocked.

A symbol that she recognized was floating in the air as a three-dimensional object. Not only did Sumi know the meaning of the symbol, but the very appearance of the thing was *known* to her.

Despite the way that the printed words on the file revealed their meanings to Sumi, neither she nor Harakin knew how to read or write. However, each of them developed their own symbol that they used to represent their names.

It was Harakin's symbol. It was flickering and slowly rotating, and it bore a similar appearance to her luminous blades.

The symbol vanished.

Can I open one of my doorways to Harakin? and before Sumi realized that the thought was in her head, one of her doors appeared. This new occurrence of them generating on their own was a mystery, but her doors now seemed to be more than they had ever been.

Sumi stepped, in the same way that she had always stepped through her doorways, but she was not able to appear at its other side. Something was preventing her from using her teleportation ability completely, yet her door still remained. Sumi tried to bring her full focus to her doorway.

Her eyes gazed at the fallen stone, but suddenly Sumi could see Harakin. She was surrounded in a pale light that looked strange.

"Harakin!" Sumi cried out, but Harakin did not respond.

Whatever was keeping Sumi from stepping through her doorway, was not preventing her from *looking* through it. She wished that she could touch Harakin's cheek, and when she reached out, she found that she could indeed do just that.

Harakin's eyes flashed open and she looked around, but she seemed unable to see anything.

"Harakin!" Sumi yelled.

Without thinking about what would happen, she grabbed Harakin's hand. Sumi pulled her through the doorway and out onto the front terrace of the destroyed castle.

Both of them were stunned.

Harakin's knees were weak, and Sumi grabbed her as she started to fall.

"Take me somewhere safe," Harakin said in a raspy voice. There was a light emanating from her neck where the royal guard had slit her throat.

Sumi knelt down with Harakin and cradled her.

I don't even know of anyplace that's safe, she thought, *or if my doorways could find somewhere like that.*

Again, as if responding to her command or desire, a doorway revealed itself to her.

"Somewhere safe," she whispered. *Bring us somewhere safe.*

Harakin and Sumi vanished.

The doorway led them to a dark space that was warm and smelled of spices and cooked food.

"Where are we?" Harakin asked in a hoarse whisper.

Someone sat up in the darkness in front of them.

"*What the fuck?!*" the person squawked.

Another silhouette shot upright and a second voice asked, "What is it, Dozi?"★

Chapter 10 – Ronging, Part Two

Ronging lurched across the grasslands with the river in sight to one side; it would lead him to the richest hunting grounds. His thoughts were a void, his emotions nonexistent. There was only the need. There was nothing left of Ronging. Ronging *was* the need.

As he got his first glimpse of the metropolis, his eyes raged with joy and desire. Its outskirts stretched north, and that was where Ronging was certain to satiate his craving. He slunk into the brush and again waited for nightfall.

The northernmost township that connected to the capital of Ruburge was Tuilii la Ru, and in those congested narrow streets, Ronging could sense his prey even now. It took all his effort to restrain himself for the last few hours. With each day that passed since his unearthly craving began to flare again, the necessity to fill it grew stronger, and the burning of his addiction had grown into a furious inferno that scorched his soul.

Slowly, evening crept over the world, and Ronging raced into the quiet town. His senses were electric, and as he drew closer, he could feel multiple photonova glands that were ripe for the taking. He just needed to find the right person, one he could overcome. Ronging knew that he was attracting attention to himself, and though he normally would have been more cautious, he rushed down one narrow street after another. His need was his guide.

It was not long before Ronging found what he sought, and all of his senses focused on the individual.

Down a shadowy alleyway, a man was slumped against the wall. He was barely conscious, mumbling to himself, and gripping the neck of a stoneware jug.

Ronging approached, leered over him, and he was unaffected by the stink of alcohol on the man's breath. The drunkard's bleary eyes moved up Ronging's weird body, and the monster grabbed him by the face and smashed the back of his head against the wall. Ronging roared, and the inebriated Shift man was no match. The creature slammed the drunkard's skull into the stones over and over until the masonry was beginning to crack, and his victim's brains were smashed like jelly.

Then Ronging froze. His entire being was honed in on the one tiny thing that could satisfy his twisted addiction. He rolled the convulsing body onto its stomach and used two of his arms to hold the man down while his third hand reached into the splatter.

Ronging dug furiously through the hideous opening in the back of the man's head, flinging chunks of brain around the alleyway. He was focused like there was nothing else in the universe except that which he sought. When his fingers found the Shift man's photonova gland, Ronging let out a peel of ecstasy and pushed himself up to his bizarre standing position. He did not even look at the tiny crystal before shoving it into the mouth he was born with, and he swallowed hard.

Pain struck, and it radiated through Ronging's bizarre body like pleasure. He screamed in rapturous agony, and it ravaged through him in morbid delight. Like the terrible beast he was, he howled up at the dark sky, as his bizarre body changed yet again.

Ronging did not wait for the new body parts to grow, the ones he knew were about to sprout from him. He headed back out to the edge of town and started off into the grasslands. His semblance of a smile, a weird distorted thing, spread across his multiple-mouthed face. Ronging wailed in ecstasy, as his transformation began.

Little bulges pushed from the flesh of his back, and his wicked laughter rang out through the quiet region east of the Ru River, as a fresh row of teeth split through his skin. They grew in a long strip from the middle of one shoulder blade to his low back. Out of the side of his face sprang one finger, then another, and then a third, and Ronging squealed in delighted torment as meaty appendages protruded from his torso in bulging mounds.

His pain subsided, and his change was complete.

The journey back to Gunge would take Ronging days⊗

Chapter 11 – Tisa & Olona, Part One

"We can't simply sneak past Gunge," Tisa explained to Olona. "If one of those monstrosities needs to satisfy its craving, it will be able to sense me immediately."

Olona furrowed her brow. "So, we need to figure out a way to make you undetectable," she stated. "Is it your mantis gland? Is that how they sense your kind?"

"I don't know much about them," Tisa replied. "Liovia was always able to see them coming in advance." She fell silent at the mention of her murdered companion.

"Is there a parts shop down in the village?"

"Parts?" Tisa asked.

"Yeah," Olona confirmed, and she pulled up her shirt on the side to reveal her ribs to Tisa, "like this."

Below Olona's armpit was a small piece of electronics the size of a coin.

"That's my double lung," she explained. "I have one on both sides. They allow me to absorb more air with each breath, and they provide me with extended stamina and endurance. I *know* that I can build a dampener for your mantis gland to get past Gunge."

Tisa looked surprised. "Oh, is that possible? And I don't know if there is a shop with what you need. I visit the village very rarely."

"I'll head into town. You don't need to come with me," Olona said. "People can be cruel to those who are different," she added with an apologetic expression.

Tisa wondered what Olona meant only for a moment, because the teenage human girl suddenly took off like a shot through the forest. Her speed gave Tisa the impression that she was a Shift.

"I'll be back soon!" Olona called before she was out of sight.

The teenager seemed very poised in her confidence, and Tisa did not know what to make of the peculiar youth. Tisa stepped into the hut that had served as her home for more than half her life. She could not have imagined leaving, but now that it was a possibility, she no longer wanted to remain in the sad little dwelling.

While Olona was gone, Tisa began to organize things that she knew they would need for the trip. She pondered why she felt so willing, not only to run off with a total stranger, but also to trust her with her very life. It seemed preposterous. If the device that the young organic mechanic constructed was insufficient, Tisa would be killed by the monsters of Gunge. She wanted to leave Xin, but she did not have any sort of plan; Tisa did not know what to do.

A short distance from Kestapoli, while still in the forest, Olona slowed her pace to a normal walking speed. She lit one of her joints and took a few pulls of smoke that she breathed out into the air above her head.

At the edge of the village, she approached a peddler and asked, "Is there a mechanic depot in this town?"

"Not a proper one," he replied, shaking his head, "but you may be able to find some equipment at the flea market down yonder," and he pointed toward a wide building a little way down the street. "There's also a small shop down in Galopis," the man added.

"I very much appreciate the information," Olona responded, and she headed to the market.

A bell rang when she entered, and a round woman with large glasses and a beaming smile called out, "Hellooo," in a singsong way.

She reminded Olona of an owl.

"I am an organic mechanic from Ruburge," Olona declared. "I came up here to help the people who were recently injured in the attack. Do you have any gear or equipment or tools for sale?"

"I surely do," the woman replied. "Not only do I keep a small collection of home-use packets in stock, I recently got a good deal on a trunk of miscellaneous and discarded parts. The at-home kits are in the jewel case behind you, and I haven't put the new trunk out on the floor yet, so let me head into the back and grab it."

"Is it heavy?" Olona asked. "I'm happy to help you carry it."

"That's mighty generous of you, girlie," the woman replied. "As a matter of fact, though, it's got wheels. I'll have it out for you in a moment." She smiled.

She turned and left Olona to examine the products that the woman regularly kept in stock. There were wound treatments, supports for broken bones, burn kits, and there were even several neutralizing tonics for venomous animals of the Infinite Waste and the vast grasslands of Xin. The glass case was well-stocked.

Olona turned to the squeaking of the trunk's wheels that foreshadowed the return of the shopkeeper and the miscellaneous parts. The woman lifted the lid, and Olona saw what was in it.

She knelt by the side of the box, and in an attempt to keep the excitement out of her voice, Olona said in an awkward monotone, "How much do you want for some of this junk?" Everything she needed was in the trunk.

"I don't rightly know. Why don't you pick out what you're looking for and make me an offer?"

Olona nodded and looked down at the contents so that the owner of the shop would not see her smile. She placed a small case onto the countertop, laid a handheld gun-style tool beside it, and she hoisted a heavy sack that she carefully placed with the other items. A little square box caught her eye, but when she opened it, it was empty.

"Too bad," Olona said to herself.

There were two rechargers that she added to her growing pile, and a collapsible exam lamp intrigued her. She debated for a moment, before placing it beside the counter. Olona also selected a few of the kits that the shop owner kept in stock. Then she made eye contact with the clerk, who seemed startled.

"You want *all* of this?"

As she was speaking, Olona placed a large stack of coins between her and the woman.

The owner's eyes shot to the money. She did a double take and quickly picked up the pile. "Done!" she declared with a grin.

"Perfect," Olona replied, "I don't suppose you have a box, do you?"

The sun was not yet at its zenith when Olona arrived back at the shack. She was surprised to see Tisa with a travel bag slung over one shoulder and an expectant expression on her face.

"I didn't know how long it would take you to build this *thing*, so I figured I should be ready to leave, whenever that may be."

"Okay," Olona replied with a determined smile, "I'll get started." She felt encouraged by Tisa's enthusiasm.

"Are you hungry?" Tisa asked.

Olona looked relieved. "I'm famished! I didn't want to impose, and I thought I might just go back to the village to get something to eat."

"I'll fix us some food," Tisa said, and the two of them headed into the hut.

Olona placed her box of equipment onto the floor beside the table, and as she spread them out before her, she described her purchases. She opened the large sack. "These are coils of multiple gauges of organowire, really quality product. This is the foundational stuff for what we do in organic mechanic work. Everything starts with this," and she held up one of the spools. Olona continued. "These rechargers allow me to work anywhere, so if one of us gets injured on the journey, I'll be able to build something to help fix us."

"The journey," Tisa whispered.

Olona looked up at her.

Tisa took a breath. "I guess I'm just…" she paused. "I don't know. I'm ready to go, but I'm nervous."

"Excited?" Olona countered.

"Maybe," Tisa replied, "maybe scared."

Olona picked up a strange device. "This will help me to make a shield for your mantis gland."

"What is it?" Tisa asked.

"It's a pressure gun. It will allow me to turn the organowire into a functional piece of machinery." Olona set up the exam lamp, activated the light, and laid a few of the premade packets onto the tabletop. "This burn kit has a packet of miteron, which is a compound developed by the Oselians. These three anti-venoms each come with their own peliophage syringes. That's another thing we can thank the Oselians for," she added. "I'll melt the metal tips from the needles and combine it with the miteron. The organowire will surround it as the internal component that will keep your mantis gland hidden." Olona gave Tisa a confident smile. "I'm going to make you a halo," she declared.

"A halo?" Tisa repeated.

"Exactly," Olona replied. She lit a joint and became focused, as she started to open packets and uncoil a little of several different gauges of wire. A cloud of smoke wisped out the door.

"I really enjoy the aroma of burning muluflower," Tisa said. "Liovia used to smoke one she called red mulu. I never cared for smoking it myself, but I liked when she did." Tears came to her eyes in a flood that she was not expecting.

Olona stood and stepped up beside Tisa. She did not say anything, but she brought her palm to Tisa's back.

Tisa wiped her eyes hard, turned to her hearth, and put a pan on the flames. She took a slow breath.

"Do you want me to smoke it outside away from you?" Olona offered.

"No, no, I really like the smell," Tisa replied. She opened a cupboard and grabbed some food items. "How did you run so fast?" she asked in a choked voice, trying to distract herself and change the subject. She tossed a few chunks of fatty meat into the pan.

"I'm not supposed to talk about it," Olona responded, but before Tisa could react, she continued. "Since you have to trust that my mechanics are going to save your life when we get to Gunge, I'll tell you all about the unregistered enhancements I've done to myself. They got me kicked out of my apprenticeship," she added with what almost sounded like pride in her voice. She took another puff of smoke.

"There are a lot of organic mechanics in the Tuilii la Ru region," Olona continued, "who don't care for me very much because of what I've done to myself." She stood and brought both hands to the backs of her legs below her buttocks. "I have mechanics in my hamstrings and quadriceps that also support my knees and hips. I've got parts in my jaw," and she touched the side of her face. "Both of my arms, my left eye and ear, the fingers of my left hand, and even the exterior of my skull under my scalp have all got mechanics." She looked playfully guilty. "I've been a naughty girl."

"Wow," Tisa replied, "and you're only 17?"

Olona shrugged. "I just *get* this stuff. It makes sense to me. It has since I was little. What I don't understand are the rules, regulations, and restrictions surrounding organic mechanic healing practices." She shrugged and got back to work. For a little while, the two did not speak.

Soon the hut was filled with the aromas of Tisa's cooking. She prepared a noodle dish with fresh vegetable florets and the rich, fatty meat. In a separate small pot, she made a thick sauce that added spicy and umami flavors to the meal.

In less than an hour, Olona constructed a strange metal framework that was almost as large as the tabletop, and the meal that Tisa was preparing was ready.

Tisa examined what Olona was building and asked, "I'm going to have to wear that on my head?"

"What? No!" replied Olona. "This is just the workstation I need in order to assemble the halo. You'll see in a little while."

Tisa held up two plates of food. "Do you want to eat?"

"*Yes!*" Olona said dramatically. "I would definitely like to eat before I get started on the real work. Erm... maybe we should eat outside," she recommended, eyeing the cluttered table.

The two women ate together in awkward silence.

After a few bites, Olona said, "This is good."

Tisa smiled and nodded.

Several minutes later, they were finished, and Olona positioned herself at the table again with the framework in front of her. She looked over her shoulder at Tisa and said, "Thank you for the food."

"You're welcome."

Neither of them spoke for the next few hours, except for the occasional mumble from Olona as she assembled several different mechanical elements, none of which looked to Tisa like a halo.

When Olona eventually said, "Finished!" she looked over with a satisfied smile. "This is some of the best work I've ever done." She sounded even a little surprised at herself.

"It's too late to start out now," Tisa said. "I'll make us dinner and we can sleep here tonight, one last time." She made eye contact with Olona and pointedly asked, "Are you sure you really just want to leave everything behind?"

"I have nothing here. My family all live to the far south, and we grew apart during my years of apprenticeship. Plus, now that I've made enemies among a bunch of the other organic mechanics, I need to find some new place to make my way. I'm good at this," Olona added, pointing at the thing that still did not look like a halo. "I know that my services will be worthwhile to someone somewhere, especially away from the regulations in Ruburge."

"But we have no idea what is…" and Tisa thought of Liovia, as she said, "northerly. We have no idea what's up there."

"And we're not going to find out until we arrive," Olona concluded. "Now, how can I help with dinner?"

The next morning, as the sun slowly began to creep up the sky, springtime birds and insects started their morning cacophony, and the rest of the world awoke.

Tisa rose, but she was alone. She found Olona buzzing busily outside of the little cabin.

"Good morning!" Olona called. "I've got the rest of what we need packed."

"We're really doing this?" Tisa asked.

Olona laughed. "Oh, you know we are! Let's eat something and head on our way."

"This is happening," Tisa said to herself.

"Yes!" Olona replied. "Are you second-guessing? Having doubts? You wouldn't be a sensible human being if you didn't have those feelings. I mean, I know you're a Shift…" but she stopped herself. "Oh, is that the right thing to call you? It's not offensive for me to call you a Shift, is it?"

Tisa smiled. "No, that's fine. I've never really thought of myself in those terms, because Liovia and I were just ourselves up here in the forest. Since we rarely went to the city, there weren't people for us to compare ourselves to. I guess I'm a Shift, but I've always just thought of myself as a person, maybe an outcast," she added.

"I've sort of always been the opposite," Olona responded. "Since there have always been loads of people around, I've always compared myself to others. My personality tends to allow me to be friends with lots of people, which can be a gift, but it actually takes a lot of effort for me to develop deep relationships with individuals," she admitted. "So I've also kind of always been on my own, even with others."

Olona leaned her pack against her lower leg and added, "I made an effort to get close with the other girls in the apprenticeship program, but there were only a few of them, and I just never really clicked with anyone. With you, Tisa," she added, "I don't know, I just want to be your friend."

"We are quite a pair," Tisa agreed. "I think I'm old enough to be your mother."

"*No you're not!*" squawked Olona. "I'm 17 and you said you're around 30ish. Maybe you're like an older sister. And I was serious," she added, almost in a pout, "I know we barely know each other, but I already feel, I don't know, close to you."

Tisa was not expecting Olona's words, nor did she know how to respond to them. She was not used to the idea of friends, and she felt herself blush. Whether out of nervousness or just a desire to change the subject, Tisa asked, "Where's the halo?"

Olona reached down and patted the bag that was leaning against her shin. "I've already packed it away. Let's eat and start walking; I think we've got a lot of that ahead of us."

Tisa was still curious about the halo. "Shouldn't we test it on me and make sure it works before we go?"

Olona looked slightly offended. "It works," she declared. "This is what I do. I *also* have to trust in the gear that I build for you, because if the monsters find you, they find me, too. I know exactly how the halo works, and I've already tested that it functions properly. Once we are close enough you can put it on. Now, what are we eating?"

"You're not worried?" Tisa asked.

Olona took a breath. "Any number of different things might happen to us, but *one* is that we might make it, might find somewhere else that we fit in that's not Xin. That's what I'm focused on," she continued, "and I acknowledge that this crazy journey we are going to take doesn't really make sense, but this is no one else's crazy journey but ours. We don't need to justify or explain ourselves to anyone."

Tisa shook her head and let out a little sigh of disbelief. "If you say so. Let's fry up some eggs."

Olona gave Tisa an inquisitive look, but she did not say anything.

"What is it?" Tisa asked her.

Olona made a guilty face. "I feel like I'm not supposed to ask," she said.

Tisa furrowed her brow and replied, "Ask what?"

Even though no one else was in the forest with them, Olona asked in a whisper, "What can you do?"

"Oh," Tisa did not seem bothered by the question, and she raised her hand. Above her fingertips, a disc of shadow appeared in the air like a hole punched out of reality. From it rose a chubby little hooded figure that spun in a circle.

"I've always been able to manifest shadows," Tisa explained. "I create these creatures. They've helped me and Liovia in the forest for years."

The thing vanished.

In under an hour, the two were turning their backs on the hut and the muddy hollow beneath the old tree, and Tisa and Olona started out along the edge of the northern forest. For three uneventful days they walked through the grasslands, and on the fourth day, Tisa decided it was time for the halo.

"How does this thing work? Is there a time limit on it?" she asked as Olona unpacked the device on a smooth stone.

It did not look like a halo. Three separate pieces of delicate machinery sat upright. They each looked more like incomplete star shapes than parts of a halo.

"That's it?"

Olona beamed with pride. "Yes! Take this piece," she instructed, handing one portion to Tisa, "and hold it in front of your forehead. I'll bring the other two pieces together and they will attach."

"Am I gonna have this metal all over my head? I mean, I don't want something eating my mantis gland but this is a bit cumbersome."

"Just wait," Olona said with excitement in her voice.

Tisa could barely see what was happening with the contraption, but a moment later, the three separate pieces slid together and clicked into place. A very dainty mechanical ring now encircled her head, very much like a tiny metal halo.

"Just right," Olona said in a satisfied tone.

"Can I touch it?" Tisa asked.

Olona smiled. "Go right ahead."

Tisa's fingers followed the thin band all the way around her cranium. "This is doing something?" she asked.

"Precisely, the halo is a dampener. At its most basic level, you can think of it as an electromagnet that's creating a field. It blocks the signature of your mantis gland from being detected," Olona explained. "It's *not* an electromagnet; it's much more complex than that, but thinking about it in terms of magnetic fields is probably the easiest way to understand it."

Tisa looked nervous. "Is there some way to test that it's working?"

Olona grinned. "I can see that it's working," she confirmed. "Not only will you be undetectable to the monsters, but if you're wearing this, I don't think anything in the world could pick up your brainwave frequencies."

Tisa frowned. "Can we walk farther to the south while we pass Gunge? Do you mind?"

With the towering mountains to the north and the sprawling grasslands as far as the eye could see to the south, Tisa and Olona began to head away from the ambiguous border to the realm of monsters. Despite that their intention was to go north, the two made their way out into the rolling lands a little way to the south, before continuing toward the sea. They were out in the open, but farther from the creatures that might murder them.

On their sixth afternoon, Olona and Tisa first saw the ocean. It took up the entire horizon.

For a moment, Tisa did not know what she was seeing. Then she gasped.

The sight of the sea brought joy to Olona. In Mellini, far to the south along the Ru River, she grew up only a short boat ride from the pink sand beaches of southern Xin.

"The ocean," Olona exclaimed in delight.

Tisa was struck speechless at the wondrous panorama that stretched out before her. She made a small sound of awe at the sight. Her eyes were wide and her mouth was agape.

"We made it," Olona said, as the sun began to set over the Infinite Waste far to the west. "Well, not *made it* as an all the way," she corrected, "made it to the sea. I haven't seen it in years, not since starting my apprenticeship."

"I've never seen it before," Tisa whispered.

Olona looked surprised and delighted. "How exciting! Let's camp nearby so we can fall asleep to the sounds of the surf."

"How far does it go?" Tisa asked. She was dumbfounded by the vastness.

Olona chuckled and replied, "All the way."

Tisa looked over at the young woman with a confused expression. "All the way to what?"

"To whatever's on the other side," Olona replied in an elated voice.

They made their camp that evening on the edge of the ocean, and Olona lit a joint as Tisa prepared a fire.

Olona exhaled a cloud of smoke and asked, "Are we cooking something?" They had eaten dried meat, fermented cabbage, and nuts for each meal on their first six days of travel, and Tisa's reply surprised Olona.

"I'm catching us a fish."

Before Olona could ask how, a disc of shadow appeared and Tisa smiled. A little figure rose from it, but then the thing took off like a shot. It entered the ocean without a splash, and for a moment, Tisa stood focused on the sea. All of a sudden, her shadow was back, and it came up with a large surge of water. Her figure was holding a dead fish.

"What..." Olona began.

"I used to catch fish in the Ru like this," Tisa explained.

Olona laughed aloud. "Well, that was amazing!" she declared. She stared at Tisa's creature of darkness as it gutted and fileted the fish, and she repeated in a whisper, "That's amazing."

Tisa took the cuts of fish and put them in a pan over the flames. Her little figure and its disc of shadow vanished.

"I'll be able to do that as long as we're close to the water," Tisa commented.

Their dinner was delicious.

The next morning, they awoke to the most beautiful sunrise that either of them had ever beheld. It shimmered off the water and painted the sky in a splendent array of colors.

"This halo is going to work, right?" Tisa asked Olona, as they ate a cold breakfast of more dried meat.

"I trust it," Olona assured her. "You can trust it, too."

"I'll trust it once we're past Gunge," Tisa muttered to herself. "Was this a terrible idea?" she asked, looking over at Olona.

"Don't say we should turn back," she replied. "I think that thought is going to come to mind, but I really feel like we should refrain from saying it. We should probably even try not to think it." Olona brought her hand to the outside of Tisa's arm. "Of course, turning around and going back to Xin is a possibility, but it does no good to think about giving up." Olona sighed. "We have no idea what's waiting for us at the end of this journey, but I've chosen to believe that whatever it is will be better than anything in all of the river lands. I'm done with Xin."

Tisa nodded in agreement. "So am I."

Under the risen sun, Tisa and Olona set off again. They turned north and followed the coastline as far from the center of Gunge as possible. The day slowly passed, and as the evening approached, the land began to rise.

Tisa and Olona were leaving the grasslands behind, and they were about to enter the thickly wooded foothills. Both of them started talking in an anxious way as they drew nearer to Gunge.

The trees were familiar to Tisa, but this was an entirely unknown region of the forest to her. She began naming plants that they passed.

"Durga pine, chiapple, whistle thistle, ogre's breath, vigortree, hair flower."

"Hair flower?" Olona interrupted.

"Yes, that, right there," and Tisa pointed.

Olona lit one of her joints and took a puff to calm her nerves. "The people of the pink sands, south of where I grew up," she started rambling, "they start smoking muluflower in childhood. I started during my apprenticeship." She took another breath of smoke and continued her nervous banter. "I imbibe it for different reasons than they do, but I was always curious about muluflower as a child."

Cliffs plummeted to the surf below, and as the evening began to darken the land, Tisa and Olona made camp at a clear patch in the trees high above the waves. They did not realize where they were that night.

As the sun rose the next morning, their elevated position gave them a clear view down into a ravine, and what they saw made their blood run cold. From the distance, they could not distinguish the individual monsters from one another that nested together in their tangled mass of flesh, but the women could see that it was moving.

Everything about the creatures looked familiar, yet uncanny at the same time, with limbs and heads and torsos and hair all jumbled in a repulsive and confusing visual. There was no way to determine how many of them there were, nor where one ended and another began, and every imaginable human skin tone was present in the amorphous blob.

Tisa and Olona realized that their vantage point also left them exposed and visible to the monsters below.

"We need to go," Tisa said in a whisper.

"I think you're right about that," Olona concurred, and they packed in haste.

Deep in the valley, one of the monsters caught sight of movement on the hill. The majority of human urges and sensations no longer existed for those Messiahs who had chosen to consume multiple photonova glands, but whether out of curiosity or just a tendency toward violence, the creature began to crawl away from its fellow beasts.

It neither informed the others where it was going nor told them what it saw, but one of its co-inhabitants was gripping it by the ankle. The one began to drag the other away from the mass, and when the second released its grip, it chose to follow the first. The two monsters made their way, each in their own unique manner, by crawling and dragging their strange altered bodies away from the encampment. They approached through a thick patch of forest and broke the tree line, as Tisa and Olona were about to head out again.

"Why are humans in our land?" one of them asked in a strange voice. It was not asking its fellow monster, nor was it questioning the two women, it was simply voicing its curiosity about the situation.

"Humans are soft," the other one stated.

The first grunted and said, "Humans shouldn't come to Gunge."

Tisa and Olona froze, and the monsters charged★

Chapter 12 – Ronging, Part Three

"Rally, you lot!" cried the commander of the Tuilii la Ru city guard. She led the charge. "Let's go!"

Five other officers from the king's guard were with her. They were all unarmed, but massive shields were strapped to each of their backs. They moved as quickly as they could with the cumbersome objects weighing them down.

"At the next cross street, you three turn and head up," she ordered half the group. "We will approach from two angles."

They split, and the squads both reached the edge of the city. Their target was ambling out into the trackless grasslands as they approached.

Ronging was oblivious to the rest of the world, delirious from the photonova gland he consumed, when three of the officers attacked him. The measly humans' assault was as pathetic as gnats, and Ronging swatted at them with his multiple arms in an absentminded way. They shoved at him with thick plates of metal, protecting themselves and perturbing Ronging; he hardly cared. Then they backed off from him.

He was still elated from the photonova gland, and in an instant, Ronging completely forgot about the annoying humans who were no longer shoving him.

Then two more irritating insects were buzzing behind him. The pair of soldiers pushed against Ronging's mutated body with their massive plate shields, and the other three reappeared and redoubled their effort.

Ronging growled from his multiple mouths, but suddenly, he was slammed by a force that he was not expecting. His bizarre body fell awkwardly, limbs flailing, and he sprawled to the ground. Pain throbbed throughout his body. His four eyes flashed with rage, and he pushed himself up, as the woman leading the attack crashed into him a second time. She kept her huge shield against Ronging and forced him in a different direction.

The commander of the Tuilii la Ru city guard once went through a brutal and secret ritual that made her powerful, and she used her increased strength to help the people of her community. She now used it to move the monstrosity toward a skinny pole with a little yellow flag.

Ronging roared and flailed at her, but she slapped his hand away with ease and kept pushing.

With a final mighty heave, the commander stopped short and sent Ronging toppling backward. He landed on a trapdoor that released, and he tumbled down into a deep circular pit, landing in mud. He pushed himself to standing. The mud came to his ankles and the sides of his prison were straight and slippery.

"And you can just rot down there," the commander said from above. She spat into the hole.

Ronging cried out in fury, but darkness enveloped him as the officers replaced the false floor above his head. They changed the flag from yellow to red and left Ronging in the pit.

He nursed the injuries that the commander managed to inflict upon him, as the hours began to slip away, and he took to exploring his tiny damp prison. He endlessly circled the chamber wall, clawing into the wet soil but unable to gain purchase of any kind.

Hours became days, and all was night in the darkness.

Ronging rarely heard anything from above, and nothing indicated to him how much time passed. With his addiction recently satiated, the only craving that he felt was to be out of the wet darkness and back in Gunge.

Days dragged into weeks, and a month slipped by with Ronging spending all of it creeping along the wet walls. Neither hunger nor exhaustion plagued him, and one month became two. Round and round he trudged through the mud, ever clawing at the walls with his multiple hands. Months slowly scraped by in mind-numbing repetition, and they eventually became a year. Still, Ronging searched for a means of escape.

In the same way that hunger and exhaustion and even breathing were no longer part of Ronging's existence, vengeance did not plague his twisted spirit. There were only two main thoughts that filled any mutated Messiah's mind. One was the addiction when it arose, and the other arrived after their monstrous desire was sated. Each inhabitant of Gunge felt an inborn pull to the others of their kind. Ronging simply wanted to go home.

Time continued its steady flow with him slogging through the mud in a perpetual circle, and the months beyond that first year kept piling up with him in the darkness. Nothing ever changed. Nothing ever happened. Ronging never found anything new.

Even when change to the monotony eventually did arrive, it was a change that was not much different from his year and a half imprisonment. As his fingers gripped the wall for purchase, like the uncountable times before, they were suddenly wetter.

Ronging could not determine the source of the additional moisture, but for the first time, the walls seemed to be seeping. Water also slowly began to rise above his ankles. Air was not a requirement for the mutated Messiah, and he did not fear the pit filling.

A horrible crack sounded overhead, as the trap door ruptured, and Ronging saw the sun for the first time since being trapped. Along with the light came a crashing muddy waterfall that rained down on his empowered form. Ronging was unharmed by the barrage, and it allowed his multiple feet purchase.

Slowly, as the floor of the pit began to rise, so did the monster within.

Ronging eventually stepped onto the land above the pit again, and he saw the cause of his liberation✪

Chapter 13 – Tisa & Olona, Part Two

The two monsters from Gunge roared and flailed their weird limbs as they charged up the incline of the land toward Tisa and Olona.

"No," Olona whispered in terror, "the halo, it's working. It is!"

Tisa put up her hands in a futile defensive position, but her otherworldly abilities responded by reflex, and something happened that startled both of the women.

Discs of shadow appeared in front of the monsters. They collided with them and the discs changed shape for a split second.

The two creatures fell to the earth. Their bodies were in pieces, and they were dead. Limbs lay on top of each other and both of their heads went rolling back down the hill into the trees. The monsters were hacked to pieces like butchered heifers, and their blood seeped into the soil.

"What," whispered Olona, "just happened?" She turned to Tisa.

"They know I'm here," Tisa said in a quavering voice. "They're after my mantis gland."

"No, they're not," Olona retorted. "At least, I don't think they are. The halo is working. They thought we were both humans and were just coming after us." Then she looked back at the dead monstrosities and commented, "With all their extra parts, it looks like there are a lot more than two bodies there." Olona then concluded, "Let's get out of here!"

They raced off along the coast and away from the mutilated mutants.

"How did you do that?" Olona eventually asked, as she lit herself a joint and took a puff.

"I don't know," Tisa replied. "I don't know what happened. I don't know what my shadows did to those things."

After the terror of the morning, the rest of the day passed uneventfully, and the two continued walking long after sundown. They decided that getting farther away from Gunge was more important than sleep that night.

For the next 67 long days, Tisa and Olona encountered no other monsters. They also did not cross paths with a single other human or Shift. Their journey was slow and difficult along the eastern edge of the vast mountains north of Xin, and the coastline they followed was rugged; it made their journey drag, but the sea provided them with food for their entire trip.

Over two months after they set out from the area of Kestapoli, under a bright sunrise, the two women saw their first signs of human habitation. Several little fishing vessels floated on the waters far to the north.

"I'm afraid to believe that it's true," Tisa stated. "Have we really made it?"

"But where have we made it to?" Olona asked.

Not long before midday, the two women reached the southernmost village of the region they entered. An old weathered sign with metal letters declared the name of the small community.

"Have you ever heard of Hazel Cove?" Olona asked Tisa.

"No, I haven't."

Olona furrowed her brow. "Does *no one* make the journey that we just did? I mean, it wasn't easy."

"I suppose Gunge is a deterring factor for people in the south," Tisa commented, "and I guess that's why we've never heard of anyone coming down to Xin from up here."

"Look, there's an inn!"

They headed for it and pushed the door open. A young woman was standing behind a desk next to a set of stairs.

"G'morning, ladies," she called. "Welcome to the Pebble Pub. What can I do for ye both?"

"We're looking for a room for the night," Olona chimed in a bright voice.

"Accommodations, we can provide. Just the two of you, is it, and just one night?"

Tisa and Olona looked at each other.

"We don't rightly know yet. Can we have the room for tonight and let you know about tomorrow night in the morning?"

"That'll be fine," the young woman replied.

Olona handed her a coin.

"Hey, what's this funny business?" she snapped. "Only real money is accepted here."

The two travelers looked at each other again.

"That's a Xinitian gold half-dollar," Olona stated. "That ought to cover…"

"*Gold?*" the woman interrupted.

Tisa and Olona looked at each other yet again.

"Yes, haven't you ever seen a half-dollar before?"

The woman took the coin, scrutinized it, and she determined that it was sufficient payment. She handed Olona a key. "Right up the stairs, turn left, end of the hall." She then asked, "Where are you two from?"

"Is there a map of the area that I could see?" Olona asked in response.

"Top of the stairs," the woman replied with a smile.

Tisa and Olona left her curious about who they were.

Sure enough, a large hand-drawn map in a wooden frame was hung on the wall.

Tisa pointed at the tiny dot at the very bottom of the map with the words *Hazel Cove* next to it.

"We did," Olona declared. "We *did* make it!"

"But where are we?" Tisa asked. "This map doesn't have a region name. Only one city and a few towns are listed."

Olona studied the image. "Maybe this part of the world isn't set up the same way as Xin."

"Hazel Cove just has a dot," Tisa commented, "and so do these other towns along the coast and in the forests. So, I think we should make our way here," and she brought her fingertip to the only star on the map. The words underneath it said *Teshon City*.

Olona nodded her head toward the end of the hall. "There's our room."

They entered it and closed the door behind them. After sliding their packs off their tired shoulders, the pair headed down the stairs and ordered a hot meal in the pub. Each of them then took the opportunity to enjoy their first bath in a very long time, and with the sun high in the sky, they drew the curtains and lay down.

Tisa and Olona slept very hard on very soft beds, and they did not wake again until late the following morning.

When Olona sat up, she pulled the curtain back just a crack and looked out the window. She groaned and mumbled, "It's still light outside, we mustn't have slept very long."

Tisa pushed herself up and rubbed her eyes. Her life away from the conveniences of the city had taught her the ability to read the time of day based on the type of light.

"No," she said, "it's morning."

Olona tilted her head to one side. "So, we slept the entire night?! I guess we needed it." She opened the curtains wider and let more light into the room. "I don't think we want to stay here. There's not much to this town. Look, you can see all of it from here." Olona leaned to one side and pointed. "There's a farm out that way; I can see the field. Oh, and there's the path leading out of town. There isn't anything else here," Olona added. "I don't think we need another night."

"I agree," Tisa said. "I've spent so many years away from people, out in the wilderness, but the time that I've spent with you has felt very…" she paused and settled on, "fresh." She gave Olona a little smile. "I'm so used to Liovia and the way she would talk about things that weren't happening, and how she was never present. I never realized that I was missing the…" she hesitated again, "companionship of other people. If you're still interested in traveling with me, I'd like to go where you want to go."

Olona looked surprised. "At this point, I can't even imagine us *not* going together! I don't know, you're kind of like the big sister I never had. I guess I sort of see us," she scrunched up her face and concluded, "as a team?"

"Yeah, I think we're a good pair," Tisa agreed.

"Why don't we head down and have some breakfast, then be on our way?"

Tisa smiled in agreement and they descended to the first floor.

"Good morning," Olona said to the young woman who was again behind the counter, "we would love some breakfast, and we've decided that we are heading back out and continuing our journey. So, we will not need a second night at your wonderful establishment." She beamed at the woman.

Less than an hour later, they were fed and making their way north with the little village behind them.

The string of fishing hamlets along the coast was set up with each village positioned a day's journey apart, and not long after sunset, Tisa and Olona arrived at Port Judy. There was no sign declaring that Port Judy was the name of the town, but a row of buildings that were already shut down for the evening each bore the name, Port Judy Hardware, the Port Judy Public Library, and the Fish Market of Port Judy.

Tisa and Olona again found a tavern, and it was called the Inn at Port Judy.

"I guess we're in Port Judy," Olona said in a nonchalant way that made Tisa snort. It was the first time Olona heard her laugh.

"Welcome, travelers," said a bearded man behind the bar. Many customers were already drinking and carrying on in the tavern. "Here for the night or just some entertainment?"

"We'd like a room please," Olona said with a smile, and she decided that it was prudent to jump straight to the topic of money. "Do you take gold?"

The man's eyes brightened and he looks surprised. "Normally I just take money," he replied with a shrug.

"Unfortunately, we have not come across the means to exchange any of our gold coinage for the standard money accepted here," Olona stated, "but at our last accommodations, they were happy to take a little gold in exchange for a room. If this doesn't work for your establishment, we understand and we'll find another place to stay."

"No, no," the man responded quickly, not wanting anyone else to receive the gold they offered him, "that'll be just fine. Is it just for a single night?"

The two women looked at each other.

"Probably," Olona replied to him. She handed the man a gold coin.

"Well, ain't that an interestin' little piece," he commented, flipping it over in his palm, but he looked pleased. "Come this way, ladies, and I'll get you your key."

After dinner, Tisa and Olona were again quickly asleep.

They arose with the morning sun, and just like the day before, they left after breakfast. Another day of travel brought them to the third fishing village, Seven Rivers, and their gold was again good at the inn. Tisa and Olona ate a decent supper, and they were soon fast asleep.

However, later that night, the innkeeper's greed overcame his hospitality. Using a skeleton key that opened any door in his building, the man crept into their room as they slept.

The two women awoke with a fright and Tisa's eldritch abilities again reacted on reflex. Her black disks appeared in the air and she could feel them take form.

There was a brief scream and it was silenced, replaced by sloppy wet sounds.

Olona flicked on the lights, and just like the two monsters of Gunge who attacked them, the man's body was in pieces. A puddle of blood surrounded the chunks that used to be the innkeeper.

"I didn't mean to do that," Tisa whispered.

Olona was staring at the body, frightened and shocked.

"I didn't mean to," Tisa repeated.

Olona asked in a stunned voice, "Was he fucking robbing us?" She pointed at one of the bloody pieces. "He was! Look, he's got my coin purse in that hand over there." It was on the floor, not attached to the wrist where it used to belong.

"But I didn't mean to," Tisa said yet again.

"Hey," Olona said, and she spoke her companion's name to help her focus, "Tisa, he was in the act of robbing us. Who knows what he intended afterward? Once he had our money, what do you think he was going to do with us? Let's just get the fuck out of here while we can."

They grabbed their things, slunk out the door, and closed it behind them with the eviscerated body oozing on the carpet.

Tisa and Olona slipped outside under the glow of the moon and headed with haste to the path that led north out of town.

They did not speak for quite a while, but eventually, Olona lit a joint and asked, "Tisa, what exactly is your power? I know you talk about them being like shadows, and I've seen them several times over our journey, but what are they?" Olona exhaled a cloud of pale grey smoke.

Tisa looked at her with a curious expression. "I'm not entirely sure," she replied, and she caused another void disc to appear right in front of her. As they walked, the shadow moved with them. It kept pace with the two women.

"I've been able to do it since my mantis gland activated," Tisa continued. "I was around 13. Liovia was the only other person I knew with any sort of abilities, and hers just sort of made her weird. I liked her, and our life together in the forest was unique, but I've never had anyone who I could really talk to about my powers," she looked into Olona's eyes, "no one who could understand or relate."

Olona blew another puff of smoke into the air above their heads, and she took Tisa's hand.

This surprised Tisa. The two women did not hold hands at any point on their journey.

"Well, now that you've got that shadow in front of you," Olona said, and she squeezed Tisa's fingers, "what can you do with it?"

Tisa took a breath and furrowed her brow in concentration. "The disks can stay there by themselves," she explained. She reached out her free hand and touched it. "But they can also become my friends." From the shadow emerged an adorable little round figure of darkness with stumpy limbs and a hood over its head.

Olona could not help but smile at the entity.

"I don't know," Tisa continued. "I used to make them carry water, or chop up food, or gather kindling, or sweep the floor. They've always sort of been my little helpers. Only a few times has my power done something..." she hesitated, contemplated the right word, and settled for, "violent." She gave Olona an uncertain look.

"Well, I'm glad they did," Olona replied. "It was not okay for that man to come into our room while we were asleep last night. You may have stopped him while he was robbing us, but I will say it again, who knows what else he had planned for the two of us? Ugh, men!"

"But I didn't mean to kill him."

Olona came to a realization. "You know what?" she said. "If he did this to us, what's he done to other people in the past? You've made it so he can't hurt anyone ever again."

The events of the night made the idea of sleep unappealing, and they continued to walk for several hours in darkness. They came to signs for Brokenpointe before they reached the village, and it was still before dawn when they arrived. A few of its inhabitants were starting to rise. Several fisherfolk were preparing their nets, and one little boat was already out on the water.

"Do we go to the inn or just continue on?" Tisa asked.

"Aren't you exhausted?" Olona replied.

"Yes, but I don't want to deal with any other dangerous people."

Olona shrugged. "You're liable to find dangerous people everywhere."

When they entered the tavern, Olona informed the innkeeper that they had traveled through the night and were looking for a room to rest in during the day and that night. He was happy to accept their gold and set them up in a private suite with its own privy chamber. After wedging a chair against the door handle for added security, both women enjoyed baths again, then they closed the curtains and fell asleep.

Tisa and Olona woke late in the afternoon, ate a filling meal at the inn, and they each ordered an after-dinner pint of ale as the sun set over the western mountains. The two women sat watching a piano player clanging out a tune and several patrons were drunkenly attempting to sing along.

Olona was the first to realize the song was a dirty one with raunchy lyrics, and she snickered at what the man sang.

"Everybody loves a good stiff fisherman's eel!"

Olona snorted.

"What's so funny?" Tisa asked.

"He is," Olona said with an embarrassed smile. "Listen."

"Slap me right on the ass with your thick fisherman's eel!"

"Oh my..." Tisa exclaimed.

"I think that I could take a few more fishermen's eels!"

Tisa let out a single peal of nervous laughter, and Olona choked on her sip of ale, as every patron in the bar suddenly joined in and sang the last line.

"Everybody loves a good stiff fiiiisherrrrmaaaan's eeeeeeeel!"

Tisa and Olona finished their pints, listening to a few more tunes, none of which had as amusing lyrics, and soon the two were back in their room. Before long, they were asleep.

After their restful time in Brokenpointe, Tisa and Olona were refreshed, and they began the final leg of their journey with the sun rising over the sea. In the distance, they could see a small lighthouse, but a stone marker indicated that Teshon City was in the other direction. They turned their backs to the blinking light and walked along the edge of a wide cove that separated the mainland from the peninsula city.

Tisa stopped and stared over the placid waters at the grand metropolis. Vast tidal flats stretched the entire distance up to a rise in the land where the massive city gates stood. This was her first time seeing a city, and it stole her breath.

Olona paused beside Tisa. "It's kind of like Ruburge."

"There're no trees," Tisa stated.

"Oh, you're right," Olona replied with surprise. "That's odd."

Tisa and Olona continued and passed the threshold of Teshon City as the sun was starting to set. They made their way into the urban sprawl and were surprised at the vibrancy of the first neighborhood they reached. Entire sides of buildings were painted with bright murals. Music was coming from multiple taverns. Street food vendors fed the masses who bustled on their many ways home as night fell and enshrouded the city in darkness.

"It looks like a lot of these little shacks," Olona said under her breath, "were just thrown together by people. Not like your hut back in the forest of Xin."

"I'll make us somewhere to live," Tisa told her, "but that will take time."

They headed into the middle of the city toward a giant stone Tower that loomed over all of the buildings. Beyond it was a region with many shops and cafes, most of them already closed for the evening.

It started to rain.

"Where are the taverns in this neighborhood?" Olona asked the city at large.

"Maybe we should have stopped back at the entrance, but there must be one around here somewhere," Tisa replied.

The rain began to fall harder, as the women came to the end of the peninsula. They gazed out at the splashing surface of Teshon Harbor. The sea beyond roiled past the stretches of mainland that reached from the north and south and protected the harbor, and each blinked with its own lighthouse.

"There!" Tisa declared, and she pointed along the coast.

A few blocks away, they could see the words *Teshon Harbor Inn*.

They were both drenched when they arrived.

"Good evening, ladies," said a mustachioed man behind the concierge desk. "Welcome to the Teshon Harbor Inn. Please, warm yourselves by our fire," he offered with a gracious wave toward a roaring hearth. "Summer rains are a rarity," he commented. "Now, how can I be of service?"

Olona ran through her spiel about not having money, but how several other establishments were willing to take gold in place of the local currency.

The man was more than happy to relieve the women of another gold coin in exchange for an entire week at the inn.

He handed Olona their room key, and she asked him, "Is there a place nearby where I can exchange my last few gold coins for the money you use here?"

The man looked unsure. "Don't rightly know," he replied. "Where are you two from?"

"Hazel Cove," Olona answered immediately.

Tisa furrowed her brow, but the man replied, "Way down south, eh? Makes sense, makes sense. Sorry I couldn't be more help. I reckon someone'll be willing to trade you some money for your gold."

Olona smiled at him.

A moment later, she and Tisa were upstairs in their room behind a locked door. It was a small chamber with no special amenities, but it was warm and dry.

Olona cracked the window and lit a joint. She blew the smoke out into the rain.

"Why did you tell him..." Tisa started, but then she looked past Olona and out the window in awe.

"That we were from Hazel Cove?" Olona finished for her.

Tisa stepped up beside Olona with her eyes wide.

"Wow," she whispered at the view.

The inn may have possessed rooms overlooking the ocean, but their window faced inland. It provided them with an incredible view of Teshon City. The buildings were black under the moonlight, and the rain continued to fall. The city held a strange attractiveness for Tisa.

"It's so beautiful," she said.

Olona smiled. "Well, this city is our new home." She put an arm around Tisa and answered her unfinished question from a moment earlier. "I figured that most people, at least most folks who are actually from Teshon City probably have not been all the way down to the little hamlet of Hazel Cove, but at least they will have heard of it and might even think of it as some faraway place."

"Oh, that's clever," Tisa replied. "You *are* clever, aren't you?"

Olona blushed and let out an embarrassed laugh. "You say that like you're surprised." She coughed a little and took another puff from her joint.

"That smells nice," Tisa commented. "Hey, I never asked you about why you smoke it. You said that you smoke muluflower differently than the other people you mentioned from the southern coast. What did you mean?"

Olona chuckled. "That's kind of hard to explain. They smoke it for what they think of as a spiritual connection, and they use it for meditation."

"What do you use it for?"

"It's inspiring," Olona replied. "There's a plant compound in muluflower that, I believe, makes me more creative with my organic mechanic practice. It really focuses me." She took another breath of smoke, exhaled it out the window, and she snubbed the end of her joint. "Hungry?" she asked Tisa.

A meal downstairs in the tavern made them both feel very sleepy, and they headed back to their room to fall into unconsciousness. Their journey was ended, but they needed a place to call home.

The next morning over breakfast, Olona recommended that they scour the city for a location. "I'm not skilled with carpentry or construction, but I'll do my best to help you build our house."

Tisa snorted a little laugh, and it made Olona smile. "It's not really going to be a *house*," Tisa replied, "although, I like that you called it *ours*. I will be able to build us a hut like the one I lived in, if we can find the lumber, of course."

Tisa and Olona finished their meal and headed out into the neighborhood.

The rain had stopped during the night, and the city was blanketed in fog. It gave the quiet streets an ethereal feel.

"Where should we start?" Tisa asked.

"It will probably be easiest on us if we find a spot that's not too far from where we're staying at the inn." Olona looked around. "Let's check out this part of the neighborhood first, and then expand our search as needed."

The two women checked down alleyways and each side street that they crossed, and they soon realized that miscellaneous debris was everywhere. Tisa pointed out a number of items that she thought might work.

"Okay, to start," she recommended, "we should build a temporary makeshift dwelling that's similar to the other shacks of the neighborhood." She pointed at a row of them. "Once we have a simple place of our own, we won't be so rushed to build something better. It'll give us the opportunity to construct a hut that we can eventually move into."

Olona looked impressed with the idea. "That sounds like a smart course of action."

The two made their way along many streets as the morning crept toward noon, but as they turned down a narrow alley that led back to the waterfront, they were suddenly face to face with a pair of old drunks.

"*Tits!*" one of them blurted out, and he grabbed Olona's chest.

"What the fuck?!" she barked.

There was a brilliant flash, and the man jolted back from Olona. He slammed into the wall and fell to the ground. He groaned, pushed himself to his hands and knees, and then vomited booze all over the alleyway.

"Wha'djoo'do?" the other man slurred at her.

Olona grabbed Tisa's hand and ran. She did not run too fast for Tisa with her mechanically-enhanced legs, but they rounded a corner and were gone. Olona did not know where she was leading Tisa, but getting away from the men was her goal.

The two women headed around several city blocks and eventually popped out at the water's edge again.

"Fucking men," Olona complained.

"What happened back there?" Tisa asked, slightly out of breath. "Why did he grab you like that?"

"Ugh!" Olona exclaimed. "So many men think women solely exist for their sake, like we're possessions. I dealt with it a bit in the apprenticeship. Men can be so fucking gross. They want to sexualize you when you're just a girl, when you're still supposed to be innocent, but then when you're old enough to *own* your sexuality, at that point they expect you to be all demure and coy. Fucking gross," she repeated.

"But what did you do to him?" Tisa asked, repeating the drunkard's mumbled question.

Olona made a sheepish expression. "I electrocuted him."

"What? How on earth did you do that?"

"This finger," Olona explained, holding up one hand, "has an organic machine of my own design that can function as a defensive weapon. It's got a volt-generator in it that I can discharge at will. I can determine how much of a shock I can give, and since I figured he was a bit numb from the alcohol, I gave him a pretty good zap." She did not sound apologetic at all. "Plus, he fucking grabbed me, and he fucking deserved what he got."

Olona looked around and added, "Where have we ended up?"

They were standing on a bare patch of stone with the harbor before them.

"This actually seems like a really good spot to build," Tisa declared, scrutinizing the area. There was a low wall nearby that was part of an old concrete structure. "We could build here. What do you think?"

Olona was already beaming. "You know construction, so I trust you in determining the right place to build, and I'll assist in any way that I can."

A light rain began to fall again.

"Let's find our way back to the inn," Olona recommended. "We can grab lunch and then hunt down some wood and whatever we'll need to start building our own little house. I think if we follow the water this way, it'll lead us back to the inn."

They did just that, making their way along the rocky coast of the peninsula, and before too long, the Teshon Harbor Inn's sign came into view. The women were not soaked, and they opted to remain in their damp clothes as they ate. Soon, they were back out in the drizzle.

"Let's head to the spot we found," Olona suggested, "and see if there are any usable materials close by that will work for building."

It took them less time than they expected to find the open flat space on the rocks above the water, and the two women began to forage the surrounding area for supplies.

"What do we need?" Olona asked.

Tisa pointed at some old wood. "Grab that busted piece of decking that's leaning up against the wall there. Oh, and look at this big piece of sheet metal. It's got some vents around the edge of it. Maybe we can use it as a roof."

There was only a single rusted bolt still holding the old piece of metal to one of the buildings. Tisa took a rock, struck the screw's head several times, and the thing snapped. As she began to dislodge the metal sheet, it turned out to be much larger than she realized.

"Olona," she called out, "leave that wood for now, and come give me a hand with this instead."

The two women finagled it free and leaned it up against the wall of the alleyway. Underneath it was an old fan inside of a metal cage, and behind it was an access doorway. It was hidden from view where the pavement was uneven beneath the ledge of an upper building.

Olona gave the fan cage a kick and said, "I bet this old thing hasn't seen the sun in 200 years!"

"And now it's exposed to the elements," Tisa commented with a shrug.

Olona added, "Let's try not to forget about *that*." She pointed with her foot toward the hidden doorway. "We can check it out sometime later."

They instantly forgot about the secret entrance behind the old fan cage.

The rain started to fall harder.

"Let's bring this metal sheet out of the alley," Tisa said. "Then we can find some more wood like that decking."

"I think we're gonna get soaked."

They both laughed, and they felt hopeful.

A little while later, much more broken decking and abandoned lumber was lying around the area they had selected, and Tisa started her construction.

"It just needs to shelter us for now, right?" Olona asked. "I recognize that it's not going to be like your hut in the forest."

"No," Tisa agreed, "it won't be anything like that, but you're right, its purpose is temporary. We just need a place to stay while we make a proper little shack, and I like this spot," she added, looking out over the water. "I think we should build our permanent home right here, too."

The rain started to pound down on Teshon City.

"Let's get out of here!" Olona suggested, and they ran back to the inn.

A few minutes later, they were in dry clothes and down in the tavern with warm bowls of stew in front of them.

"Mighty peculiar weather we're havin' this season," the barkeep informed them.

"Quite," Olona replied vaguely. She then asked, "Is there a store nearby that sells quality lumber and tools?"

The man scratched his stubbly chin and looked down the bar. "Oi!" he called out to another fellow who was cleaning goblets. "Where's that there wood shop?"

"Corner of 16th and Waters Way!" he hollered back.

"Corner of 16th and Waters Way," the barman repeated.

Olona chuckled. "Thanks, we'll find it."

He smiled and headed back to the kitchen.

The rain stopped that evening and did not return.

Tisa and Olona spent the next three and a half days constructing their temporary shack. They visited the wood shop several times and purchased some tools and a little lumber, but most of what they used, they found in the city. When the walls were complete and sturdy, they put the metal sheet onto the top, and Tisa and Olona stepped back to admire their work.

It was an ugly shanty that looked like every other ugly shanty in Teshon City, and it was perfect.

Both of them slipped in through the door. It was large enough to stand upright or lay down stretched out, and it was theirs. This new rickety home may have only been an empty square box with a metal roof, but Tisa and Olona felt an excitement and invigoration at all the possibilities that their new life in the city held.

They stayed at the inn for the rest of the time that Olona's gold got them, and during the days, they built a bed for their shack and made a mattress that they stuffed with straw.

On their sixth morning, Olona told Tisa, "I think it's my birthday."

"Oh, well, happy birthday," Tisa replied. "You aren't sure?"

"They don't seem to track dates up here the same way that people do in Xin. The months are all different and theirs don't have the same number of days." Olona brought a hand to the back of her neck with an embarrassed smile. "Anyway, I think that my birthday is around today. Erm… do you want to share a bottle of wine with me tonight?"

"Like a celebration?" Tisa asked.

"Yeah," Olona laughed nervously, "my mother used to let me drink wine spritzers on special days."

"What's that?"

Olona smiled as she reminisced. "It's just wine and sparkling mineral water, not too exciting, but it made those special days feel special."

That night, they spent an extra gold coin on a very large dinner and a fancy bottle of bubbly wine. The tavernmaster also plated up two wedges of chocolate cake that was not on the menu.

"I make this special for a few regulars," he informed them, "but most folks don't know about it." He wore a beaming smile, as he set down their desserts and cleared their empty dinner plates.

After the busy initial week in the city, Tisa and Olona spent their first night together in their new home. It was not much, but it was theirs.

The next few days passed in a blur of activity as both women found their bearings in the neighborhood. The locals referred to it as the Spritehood.

Olona fit right in and made fast friends with little effort, but Tisa struggled with the difference in city life compared to everything she had experienced with Liovia in the forest. Making friends was difficult for her, and she spent much of her time alone in the little hut.

Tisa filled her days with woodworking, improving the interior of their home, and building pieces of furniture for their more permanent dwelling. She constructed a new bed that stood upright against the wall when they were not using it, so that it was not taking up space during the day. Tisa also built a small table and a chair for each of them. She even cut out windows from two of the walls that gave them a view out over the harbor.

Days became weeks, and weeks stretched into a month, and Tisa told Olona that they could eventually move into their new home. Tisa was sure that she was finally going to thrive, now that she was done planning their permanent hut, but she continued to struggle with her life in the urbanscape.

Tisa made many attempts to fit in with the inhabitants of Teshon City. She even abandoned her clothes from the forest and took to dressing in the local style, hoping it would help her fit in and make friends. Over the following few weeks, Tisa spent much of her time alone. Eventually, her anxieties and disappointments began bubbling up in outbursts of frustration.

"I should never have come here!" she declared one day.

Olona heard Tisa say things like this from time to time, and for a while, she tried to share words of encouragement during those darker moments. After some time, she took to staying quiet and allowing Tisa to vent.

"I hate this city. I hate the fact that I can't seem to get my life here off the ground. I hate the way I feel around crowds, and I hate most of the people with whom I've interacted. I don't know what I'm supposed to do." Tisa dropped her head, and she cried out in exasperation. "Argh! I think I'm allergic to this city!" She let out a breath and added in a dejected tone, "This was a mistake. I should never have come here," she repeated.

Those initial impressions of awe that Tisa felt at her first sights of Teshon City were now far from her mind.

Whatever obligations may have required Tisa's attention that day were going to be ignored. She said, "I'm headed out."

This was a normal reaction in her more frustrated moments.

Tisa walked down several streets, turned a few corners, and she began to wander. In the weeks since they had arrived in Teshon City, Tisa had explored all of the Spritehood, and she now made her aimless way along streets she knew well, trying to work off her anxiety. She headed to where the edge of the neighborhood bordered the old Oselian base barracks, then she made her way in toward the center of the city. Tisa turned onto a street she did not recognize, and a moment later, she realized that she was at the edge of Gate Town.

The vibrant murals and exuberance of this very different neighborhood drew Tisa into it. After a few streets, she came to a narrow alley where she saw a pile of old lumber that she considered a jackpot. There was a large overhang protecting the space where the wood was piled. Only the bottom pieces were spoiled with a little damp from the concrete; most of it was in pristine condition.

Tisa knelt down to go through the pieces, and a voice behind her mumbled, "You're one."

A man was seated on a rickety stool a little farther into the alleyway. He was clutching a stoneware jug and took a swig from it. Several small shacks stood beyond him in the deeper shadows.

Tisa stood upright and turned to face him. "One what?" she asked.

"One of me!" the man declared with a goofy grin. There was a violin at his feet.

"Alright," Tisa said, "have a nice day." She picked up a few pieces of wood.

As she began to head out of Gate Town, the man said, "Not that way."

Tisa turned back to him and asked, "What do you mean? Why not?"

"They don't like me out there," he said. "They barely like me in here." He nodded toward the rest of Gate Town. He took another gulp from his jug.

"Look, friend," Tisa started.

"Tilby," he stated.

"What?"

The man repeated himself. "Tilby, I'm Tilby."

"Tilby," Tisa obliged, "I need to go."

"I shouldn't go that way!" he cried out with more concern in his voice than Tisa expected. "I don't belong out there!"

"I'm not asking you to come with me, Tilby," she explained. The man was obviously inebriated, but living with Liovia was often like being around an inebriated person, and Tisa was patient. "I'm just going home," she told him.

"Oh, no, *no*," Tilby wailed, "I don't live out there!"

"It's okay," Tisa comforted. "You don't have to go anywhere. You can stay right where you are."

"But I'm *leaving!*" Tilby implored.

Tisa put her wood back down. "What's wrong?" she asked him. "What are you afraid of?"

He took another draught from his oversized bottle and gave Tisa a scrutinizing look. "You're one of me," he declared, and he took another drink.

"If I am you, are you *me*?" Tisa asked, and she continued. "Are you saying that you're worried about me leaving and going that direction?" She pointed out of Gate Town.

Tilby's face broke with concern again. "I can't go that way!"

"Okay, okay," Tisa said in a calm voice. "You don't want me to go out there; I get it."

Relief washed over his face, and he went to take another swig of his booze, but Tisa reached out and put her hand on his wrist. Tilby lowered his jug to the pavement and looked up at her with bleary eyes.

Tisa asked him, "What are you trying to protect me from?"

He leaned toward her and whispered, "You're one." Tilby squinted his eyes shut, and within Tisa's mind, she suddenly heard the man's reverberating words.

You're one! and his voice in her head sounded very powerful.

His brow relaxed, and he whispered with a smile, "You're one."

"How did you do that?!" Tisa asked in awe.

Tilby's smile widened. "*I'm* one." He looked at her expectantly and he picked up his violin.

"But I can't do that," she told him.

He closed his eyes again, and Tilby's voice echoed *I am one!* in her head. He opened his eyes and repeated yet again, "You're one."

"Are you..." Tisa began, and she hesitated. "Are you asking what I can do?"

Tilby exclaimed, "You're one! You're one!"

"Okay, okay," Tisa replied again. "I can make shadows," she informed him.

Tilby told her, "It is my *most* unique," and then he stopped speaking and gave her a toothy smile, but Tisa thought he did not finish whatever he was saying. "I am not afraid," Tilby added, placing his palm on his heart. He then extended his other arm towards Tisa, as if to do the same to her, and he repeated himself. "I am not afraid."

Tisa was used to trying to make sense of confusing words. "Are you saying that I shouldn't be afraid of my shadows?"

Tilby's face was drunkenly delighted, and he picked up his violin and its old frayed bow. He dragged it across the strings and played a single chord. It sounded scratchy.

Tisa raised her hand and opened a void in the atmosphere like a disc of shadow.

Tilby gasped aloud in amazement, and he whispered, "The radiation of the universe! Stars and time and distant galaxies!"

Tisa did not understand and was taken aback by the man's sense of wonder. Her disc of darkness disappeared.

Tilby sighed, as if a lovely piece of music had just finished playing. Then he played his own, dancing his bow over the strings in a merry jig. He lowered his instrument, hiccupped, and took another swig from his jug.

"I've got to get out of here, but I'll come back tomorrow," Tisa told him. "Any chance you might sober up a little?"

Tilby suddenly looked defeated. "This is how I keep the other voices away," he said in a downtrodden tone. "So loud," he murmured. His eyes shut, and he rubbed his head as if in pain.

"It's okay; it's okay," Tisa assured him. "Don't worry, do what you need to do. I can't stay any longer now," she added, "but I'll be back tomorrow." She picked up the lumber and began to leave Gate Town, but Tilby cried out again.

"I can't go that way!"

"I know," Tisa said gently. "I get it that you don't want me to go back to the Spritehood, but that's where I live. That's where my home is."

"I can't live there! I can't live there!" Tilby started repeating. "I can't live there!"

"Why not?!" Tisa said loudly to interrupt him, but then she continued in her calm voice. "Why can't you go to the Spritehood?"

"Because they're looking for me," he said, reaching out to her again. "They're looking for *me!*" and Tilby pointed at her.

"Someone's looking for me in the Spritehood?" Tisa asked.

He looked relieved again.

"But there's no one after me," she continued. "I've lived there for weeks, almost two months."

"I can't live there anymore!" Tilby declared with a horrified expression on his face. "They were even hunting me here!"

"Look," Tisa interrupted again, "I think I understand. You think someone is after me, and I shouldn't live in the Spritehood, but I don't understand who would be after me."

"They're after me," he said again.

Tisa sighed. "You're the first other person I've met who's like me," she informed him. "I need to get back to my home, but I'll come here tomorrow. I know you don't want me to go," she added before he could argue about her leaving Gate Town, "but I'll be back," she reassured him. "I'll be back tomorrow."

That night in their tiny house, Tisa told Olona about her encounter.

"His name is Tilby, and I think he's got some sort of ability like Liovia. It seemed like he really wanted me to move into Gate Town, which makes me wonder if he's privy to something we don't know."

Olona thought for a moment and said, "Folks up here commonly call people like you *Shifts*," she explained. "Down in Xin there are a few vulgar names for your kind, and I think mostly our people just don't talk about Shifts, which is why I was worried that calling you *Shift* might be an insult." Olona smiled and continued. "But that's what you are, and I know you've made our house really amazing," she added, waving her arms at their home, "but for the past few days, I've been thinking that we might need to leave it behind."

Olona went on, "I've made acquaintance with quite a few people, including several alchemists and mystics and Demifae, and I've recently learned that it's common practice here for people to hunt your kind. They kill Shifts and use their mantis glands for any number of things. I didn't know that was how Demifae did their magic, and I think we do indeed need to move," and Olona added, "for your safety more than anything."

The next day, Tisa returned to the alleyway and found Tilby outside his shack.

"Well, I think I figured out what you were talking about yesterday," she told him. "My friend and I are going to move to this part of town where it's safer. I can't stay and chat right now, because she's already packing some of our things, and I need to get back to help her. We'll be moving somewhere in the area, and I'll come chat with you more later when I know where we are going to stay."

Tilby could not have looked more pleased, and he exclaimed, "I'm moving out of the Spritehood! I'm moving out of the Spritehood!"

Tisa laughed. "Yes, yes, I'm moving out of the Spritehood."

He joined her laughter and extended his jug toward her. The contents sloshed around inside.

Tisa held up her hand. "Thank you," she said with a smile, "but I've got a lot of moving to get through today, maybe another time." She nodded to him and headed back out of Gate Town.

She met up with Olona, and for the rest of the day, they scouted locations in Gate Town. To their surprise, they found an old Oselian building that was empty. It stood right on the border of Shifton. They spend the next few days making trips back and forth with the things Tisa built for their shack by the water, and soon, they were settled in a new home.

Time continued its steady flow, and life felt a little more bearable for Tisa in an area surrounded by her fellow Shifts, even if most were still living in secret. She still struggled to make friends, but there was a new peace in her heart.

During the following six months, Olona was constantly engaged in many different activities, and Tisa spent a lot of her time in the alleyway with her confusing new friend. Tilby reminded Tisa of Liovia, and she enjoyed being with the peculiar fellow.

Tilby would say things like, "I wonder what I can do," and, "How many can I make at once?" He also told Tisa things like, "My shadows are so wonderful," and, "I love them so much!"

His words were encouraging to Tisa, and it did not take long for her to start experimenting with her discs of darkness and testing her abilities. Tilby laughed at the appearance of her little chubby hooded figures. He was amazed by the entities' ability to manipulate physical objects, while themselves being nothing more than shadow.

"I hear the radiation of the universe! I taste the stars! I see time and distant galaxies!" Tilby often said different variations of those confusing lines, and Tisa liked it when he did.

Their pleasant experiences together were countered by the villainy that eventually became apparent. Living in Gate Town was in some ways safer, and in other ways more dangerous.

Gate Town was the primary hunting ground for those who desired Shift photonova glands. The people who lived in that region were more sympathetic to the plight of the hunted, and they were accepting of the existence of Shifts. In the daytime, there was usually safety around other people.

The city nights were different.

Over their first six months in Gate Town, Tisa and Olona were told about Shifts who were hunted down. They overheard rumors about isolated cults outside the city, and Olona even stumbled upon the headless corpse of a young woman in an alleyway. The Shift owner of a cafe that she and Tisa often visited went missing one day, and he was never found. During that half-year, nine different neighbors of theirs turned up dead and decapitated or disappeared altogether.★

Chapter 14 – Ronging, Part Four

Every several years, the winter snows fell heavier on the mountains north of Xin, and the subsequent spring thaw caused the great Ru River to overflow its banks. Most houses built in the region were constructed on tall stilts that were sunk deep into the earth. They allowed the flooding to freely flow beneath the homes without destroying them.

Much of the inhabited land near the river was currently under several inches of water. The flood was vast, and the pits that the people of Tuilii la Ru dug in the dry years to catch and imprison the monsters of Gunge were filled with water.

In the interim since the last flooding of the Ru River, Ronging was the only creature to hunt for a photonova gland in that township, and he was their only prisoner. Once the unguarded hole was full and he was free, he turned his back on Tuilii la Ru and began to lumber out into the sprawling grasslands. With his addiction still satiated, his only urge was to return to his own kind.

Ronging was unpursued, and he trudged back toward Gunge✪

Chapter 15 – Tisa

On an unimpressive day that was very similar to many of the days before it, for one brief moment in time, everything went horrible for Tisa.

It was a chilly evening at the beginning of her first winter in Teshon City, and the sunlight was swiftly fading.

Tisa was collecting boards in an alley when a pack of hunters descended upon her, and she was trapped. Like holes that led to oblivion, her shadow discs suddenly surrounded her, and the headless skeletal torsos that emerged from them were terrible.

Tisa spoke, "I can hear the cosmic music from the radiation of the universe!"

Before the first would-be attacker could get to her, one of Tisa's creatures lashed out with a vicious sword comprised of nothing but darkness. It cut cleanly through the man's neck and severed his head from his body.

Tisa continued, "I can taste the elements that burn in the stars!" and she sounded like a goddess.

"Claw Two, watch out!" someone cried from the mouth of the alleyway, but it was too late.

Another terrible apparition from one of Tisa's disks of darkness appeared, and it swiped through the air with a curved blade. Claw Two's forearms were lopped off just above the elbows, and the woman fell to the ground, writhing and screaming. Her cries of anguish became a quiet gurgle, as she was skewered by another entity of shadow that impaled her to the ground with a brutal spear.

Headless skeletons of darkness were now protruding from each of the void discs.

"I see the world!" Tisa declared, and her voice came not only from her own mouth, but also from every one of her entities that filled the alleyway. Her words echoed with furious wrath. "I can see eons!"

One of her creatures struck another hunter with a brutal club, and a blade of blackness bit into the man's hamstrings. He crashed to the pavement and roared in agony, as he tried to drag himself away from the deadly encounter.

Tisa wreaked havoc against her unknown enemies. "I look into distant corners of alien galaxies!" she cried, expounding on thoughts shared with her by Tilby.

Horrible weapons of darkness cleaved three more assailants, as they attempted to strike out at the hideous headless monstrosities. Their blows passed through Tisa's shadows, but they were so much more than shadows. The swords and spears from the void also passed through the hunters, and their bodies fell to the grimy gutter, mangled and dead.

The hamstrung man was the only one left alive in the alley. He was trying to crawl away from the oncoming death, and he was wailing.

Tisa stepped up and stood over him.

"Where are the others?" she asked, but she did not wait for a reply.

Another shadow hole opened and a vaporous skeletal form appeared with a massive battle-axe clutched in its bony fingers, and the creature brought its blade down on the man's ankles like a guillotine.

As his feet were removed from his legs, the man let out a scream like a lobster being boiled.

"Where are they?!" Tisa asked again.

"*Fuck you!*" he spat.

Without hesitation, her darkness monster struck again with the force of an avalanche.

The man shrieked, as both his legs were chopped through the knees.

"Who's out there?" Tisa snarled at him.

The man bawled, "*Talon!*" and he reached for his leader.

"Who is that? Where's Talon? *Where is Talon?!*"

Her creature struck again, but this time, its blade sank through the meat and bone of the hunter's shoulder and took off his entire arm.

Bleeding out in the alley at Tisa's feet, the one-armed and legless man whimpered pitifully. With his remaining limb, he reached forward and pointed a quivering finger at a rooftop several buildings away.

Tisa looked up and saw another man. He was staring straight at her, and even at the distance, he appeared shocked.

A final strike of the battle-axe removed the dying man's head from his shoulders.

Tisa had never attempted conjuring one of her creatures at a distance, but when she reached into her powers, they obliged. Another disc of void appeared in a flash of darkness several stories up, right in front of the man who was staring at her. A headless skeletal entity emerged with a spear, and it thrust its weapon into the man's heart.

As the last hunter fell from the rooftop, Tisa withdrew all of her apparitions.

She was alone, surrounded by death, and she knew this was right. Tisa wondered what it would all mean for her, as an idea began to percolate in her mind, and she was certain of the potential of her idea.

The day after her encounter with the hunters, there was the attack on the Teshon City underground. She did not learn about the incident until it was over, but the news of the battle helped Tisa recognize the purpose behind her new idea. However, it would be a full year before she was able to put her plan into action.

On one cold night, Tisa and Olona stood among the resistance in Gate Town. The crowd was protesting a group of Messiahs who were insistent upon imposing their authority over the city. There were many Shifts in the resistance, some of whom Tisa came to know over her year and a few months in Teshon City. There were other humans, like Olona, who befriended their Shift cousins and lived with them. Present also were several Biological Shifts, and although their unusual appearance always startled Tisa, she was grateful they were with the resistance. She always enjoyed seeing any of them in Shifton.

A bear-man growled insults at the Messiahs to one side of her. He was huge, towering over most of the crowd, and thick dark fur covered every inch of him. Tisa's eyes kept shifting in his direction, but the Messiahs who were opposing the resistance were her main focus. They menaced with clubs and blades and all sorts of weapons, but when a blue light began to emanate from the bear-man's eyes, Tisa turned her gaze back to him.

She could feel the oncoming confrontation, and she was ready to add her powers to the protection of all other Shifts in Gate Town, but when the clash finally happened, Tisa was almost instantly incapacitated.

A blast of blue energy sent the neighborhood spinning into chaos.

Tisa managed to conjure only a single void disc among the group of Messiahs. A vicious bolt of black fire blazed from it at the invaders of Gate Town. However, before she was able to do anything more, a massive chunk of stone came hurtling through the air. It exploded against one of the old Oselian military buildings in a spray of concrete shrapnel, and one of the chunks collided with the back of Tisa's head, knocking her out cold.

The battle erupted so quickly that Olona did not have time to get involved in the violence before Tisa fell to the pavement.

"Let's get the fuck out of here!" Olona yelled to her unconscious companion. She grabbed Tisa under her arms and dragged her away from the fighting. Olona's mechanically-enhanced body pulled Tisa with ease, and in a matter of minutes, the two women were back in their home at the edge of Shifton.

Olona immediately treated the small wound on the back of Tisa's head. She cleaned it and applied a thin layer of ointment, then wrapped her head in a bandage. Olona tried to wake Tisa by speaking her name and gently patting her cheek, but the terror she had felt when the battle started now overwhelmed her, and she broke down in sobs that shook her body. Olona brought her face to her hands, and she cried hard.

Then fingers gently caressed her arm.

Olona looked up at Tisa through her tears.

"What happened?" Tisa groaned.

Olona shook her head. "It was really bad," she whispered. "People were dying. I was scared, and I got you out of there."

Tisa's brain was bleary from the blow. "My head," she moaned.

"Yeah, you got hit with a rock. Hey, don't mess with the bandage!" she commanded, as Tisa began to tug at the fabric. "Just relax," Olona said in a gentle voice. "Lay with me. Tell me about Liovia. What was it like living with a witch? By the by, I'm glad you're okay," Olona added. She climbed onto the bed behind Tisa and wrapped her arms around her injured companion.

Tisa mumbled, "She wasn't a witch."

"I know," Olona said with a smile. She was very glad to be home.

They stayed up late and talked for many hours, as the adrenaline in their veins and brains dissipated. Tisa told stories about her life in the woods, and Olona shared her disappointments from her time as an apprentice. They each talked about their past many times before that night, but returning to the familiar topic comforted them before they eventually fell asleep.

That was the night that the Messiah Tower was destroyed.

Tisa went looking for Tilby many times after the Battle of Gate Town, but she never found him again, and she never learned what became of her friend.

A few months later, while Tisa was home alone, a bizarre machine materialized before her. She was startled by its appearance, but even more so, she was intrigued. On the front of the machine, several components shifted into a square that extended forward from its surface, and the shape of a human hand appeared. The hand began blinking with a soft yellow light.

Tisa pondered for a moment, but then she brought her palm to the illuminated handprint.

She and the machine vanished.

They instantly reappeared in a dark underground chamber, and a voice spoke behind Tisa.

"It looks like Tualu has decided to add a new member to our team."★

Chapter 16 – Home

A pale light was still emanating from the wound in Harakin's neck. Her voice sounded harsh and raspy in the quiet darkness. "Are we safe?" she asked. She looked up at Sumi's face, which was illuminated by the faint glow.

Sumi was cradling her.

Dozi and Ilya looked at each other.

"Safe?" asked Ilya.

Dozi lit a candle.

"Where are we?" Harakin whispered.

Instead of answering, Dozi spoke up, "How did you get in here?"

Ilya ignored her. "What did you mean *are we safe*? Did something happen? Where did you come from?"

Harakin's head dropped and the light from her neck died.

Dozi's eyes went wide, and she leapt to her feet. "Ilya, the mystic's wound patch!" she ordered, as she rushed to Sumi's side. "Bring me more candles!" she demanded. "It's a deep cut. I need his pilipili ointment!" she called to Ilya. Dozi then looked into Sumi's eyes. "What's your name, girl?"

"Sumi," she replied in a frightened voice. It felt like Harakin's life was slipping away, and there was nothing she could do.

Ilya stepped up behind Dozi. "Here!" She handed Dozi the patch.

"I need more light!" Dozi barked.

"Got it!" Ilya replied.

A moment later, several candles were burning.

With careful precision, Dozi spread the ointment over the terrible wound. She laid the patch over it and wrapped Harakin's neck in a long bandage strip.

"Put her on my bed," Dozi commanded.

Sumi stood, holding Harakin in her arms, and gently placed her on the cot. Dozi spread a blanket over her, and Sumi could not stop a sob that choked its way up her throat. Tears welled in her eyes.

"Come on, Ilya!" Dozi snapped. "We're not done here! Is that dispenser set up yet?"

"Almost!"

"Hurry up!"

"She's lost so much blood," Sumi managed between shuddering breaths. The emotions that she always felt toward the cruel medics back at the compound began to prickle in the back of her mind.

However, as she watched the two young women treating Harakin, there was something unfamiliar happening in the shadowy basement. It was something Sumi was not used to, something she had forgotten.

Dozi and Ilya cared.

Although they were shouting at each other in a jarring way, and Harakin and Sumi may have both been complete strangers, the two of them were trying to save Harakin's life.

"Get the tube connected!"

"Where's the clamp?"

"Wheel that thing over here!"

"Move it out of the way!"

Dozi reached down to Harakin and released the top few buttons of her shirt.

"What are you doing?" Sumi managed to ask. She felt the urge to step in and stop Dozi from disrobing Harakin while she was unconscious.

"We need to apply this directly over her heart," Dozi explained. She indicated things as she spoke, none of which Sumi recognized. "The alchemical potion, here, will run down this tube for the next hour, and she'll slowly absorb the medicine through her skin."

Sumi was uncomfortable with what she was hearing. "That's not how the medics treat us. What if it hurts her?"

"What medics?" Ilya asked.

Sumi looked at Dozi, then at Ilya. "We are…" she began, but her voice went up at the end like a question, "soldiers."

The constant threat of torment stole much of Sumi's free will while living at the compound, but in the basement, her mind started moving like lightning. She was never given the opportunity to feel hope, and Sumi thought about the nature of her existence for the first time.

As Dozi and Ilya finished their care for Harakin, they left her sleeping and brought Sumi into the kitchen.

"We can't go back," Sumi whispered, and she looked toward Harakin. "We were taken from our families, a long time ago. They make us do bad things there. We can't go back," she repeated.

"Can't go back where?" Ilya asked.

Sumi furrowed her brow. "There are officers, a commander, prisoners, the medics," she listed. "It's underground. We can't go back!" she repeated with more urgency.

"We are not going to make you go back," Ilya replied. She reached out and put her hand on Sumi's arm.

Sumi flinched, but that did not stop Ilya from gently taking ahold of Sumi's limb in a gesture of affection that was entirely foreign to her.

Dozi pointed back toward her bed and asked, "What's her name?"

"Harakin," Sumi replied.

"Can you tell us how you got here?" Ilya asked in a gentle voice.

Sumi nodded and answered, "I can make doorways. They let me go from one place to another."

"You're a Shift?" Dozi asked.

"I don't... I don't know what that is," Sumi responded.

Dozi and Ilya looked at each other.

"How do you not know what a Shift is?" Dozi asked.

"*I'm* a Shift," Ilya said, and she activated her powers. Her feet lifted off the floor of the basement, and she hovered with a smile on her face.

Sumi looked dumbfounded.

Ilya planted her feet back on the ground.

"*I can't do that!*" Sumi declared.

"No, no," Ilya replied with a chuckle, "each Shift is unique. *I* can fly."

"Can she do something?" Dozi asked, and she tested her name. "Harakin?"

Sumi turned her astonished gaze from Ilya and nodded at Dozi. "Yes," she answered, "Harakin can make blades out of light. I've never seen a wound glow like her neck was glowing though. That was..." she paused, "weird."

"So, wait, how did you get here?" Ilya asked again.

"I made a doorway, but I don't know why it brought us here." She looked back at Harakin. "Thank you for helping her," Sumi whispered.

The three women stood in silence for a moment.

"By the by, I'm Ilya and this is Dozi. Did you two come from somewhere outside of Teshon City?"

Sumi looked puzzled. "I don't know what that is."

"Teshon City?" Dozi asked. "*This* is Teshon City. We live there, or rather, here. You're in it."

"I've never heard of it before. The compound is near the Ru River."

"The compound?" Ilya asked.

"The Ru River?" Dozi added.

Sumi was confused. "You don't know the River? It's the lifeblood of Xin."

Dozi and Ilya made eye contact again.

"*Shin?*" Dozi asked.

"Erm... Xin," Sumi repeated in her accent, "it's where we're from." She looked over at Harakin again, and her eyes lingered on her only friend in the world.

"I've never heard of Xin," said Ilya, testing the word. "Is that a village located somewhere in the forests or mountains that surround Teshon City?"

"*What?*" Sumi was bemused and her head was spinning. "I... I don't even know what you mean."

Ilya decided to give the newcomer a break. "Are you hungry?" she asked. "Would you like some food?"

Dozi followed Ilya's lead. "Yeah, let's throw something together and let her sleep." She indicated Harakin and handed Sumi a cold meat pie. "Start with that," Dozi added, "and I'll make something hot." She put a frying pan on her single-burner stove as Sumi took a tentative bite.

Her eyes began to sparkle, and she took a much bigger bite. "What issh thissh?" she asked with her mouth full. She sounded astonished.

"It's just a meat pie," Dozi said with a dismissive shrug.

Ilya was scrutinizing Sumi. "You've never eaten something like this?"

"The only thing," Sumi mumbled with her mouth absolutely stuffed with meat pie, "they ever gave us," she swallowed, "was carbohydrate bars and protein gruel, nutrients sufficient for what they made us do." She looked over at Harakin and tears came to her eyes again.

"It's okay," Ilya comforted. "We're not going to make you do anything; don't worry. And meat pies are a common dish here. Dozi's are good, though, aren't they? But hey, you can relax a little. You're safe here," she added.

Dozi looked up from the frying pan and over her shoulder at Sumi. She gave her a warm smile and a small nod. "This place has been home to a number of us strays over the time that I've lived here." Dozi then turned all the way around and looked over at Harakin. "Sumi, if you two need a place to stay, you can stay here with us for as long as you want," Dozi offered.

Ilya smiled at Dozi and added, "Welcome to Teshon City!"

A few hours later, Harakin began to stir, and she sat up. She brought her hand to the bandage on her neck.

"Careful," Ilya said in a quiet voice, "don't mess with that."

Harakin looked over at her and murmured, "Where's Sumi?"

"I'm right here!" Sumi called, coming out from Dozi's kitchen area. "I'm here," she repeated softly. "You're safe. Somehow, we're not in Xin anymore; my doorway took us to a completely different part of the world. This is Dozi and Ilya," she added. "Neither of them has ever heard of Xin. We're in a place called Teshon City."

"That's a lot of information to lay on someone who just woke up," Dozi commented. She turned to Harakin. "Are you okay? How do you feel?"

Harakin furrowed her brow. "Weak," she replied.

"Do you want some food?" Dozi offered.

Harakin nodded.

Ilya jumped up and grabbed one of Dozi's meat pies. "Here you go," she said, handing it to Harakin.

"You need to regain your strength," Dozi encouraged. "We've been chatting with Sumi, and when you're up for it, we'd like to take you to see some friends. One of them is a healer who can provide you with better treatment for your neck. That's just temporary," she added, indicating the bandage.

Harakin nodded with her mouth full. She also seemed amazed by the simple meat pie.

"Sumi told us about where you came from," Ilya said. "It sounded horrible."

"Dozi's offered us a place to stay here with her and Ilya," Sumi informed Harakin. "We never have to go back," she said in a choked voice, as a lump rose in her throat. Tears threatened to spill from her eyes again.

Dozi nodded. "I'm sorry for everything you've been through, and look, this city can be tough, but at least you'll be able to make a life for yourself. Sumi told us that you were made to feel like you don't belong around people." She looked over at Ilya. "We both think you've simply met the wrong sort of people."

"Yeah," Ilya agreed, "I'm a Shift, too. For a long time, I kept myself hidden, but now I'm part of a family."

Between bites, Harakin asked, "What's a Shift?"

"*We* are," Sumi replied. "That's what they call people like us in this part of the world."

Harakin frowned. "I didn't think there *were* any other people like us."

Dozi interjected. "Erm... I'm not actually a Shift," she said. "I'm just a boring old human."

Ilya gave her a playful slap. "Don't say that!" she said with a smile. Ilya turned to Sumi and Harakin. "Our neofamily is made up of several Shifts, like us, a few *wonderful* humans, like Dozi here, a couple of ex-Messiahs, and even a Bio-Shift!"

"They're all good people," Dozi confirmed, "accepting people. Once you've finished eating, we can head over to the mystic's place so he can give your wound proper care."

Sumi perked up and asked, "Mystic?"

"He's a healer," Ilya explained. "He lives with his husband and daughter in Shifton. They used to live over here near us, but they moved more than a year ago. Tchama is another friend you'll get to meet. She lives with them, too."

"She used to live here in the basement with us," Dozi added, "but she was injured a few months ago during a battle, and it's been easier for her to stay with the mystic while she relearns how to do some things."

Harakin finished eating while listening. Then she informed the others, "I think I'm ready to go see him."

The four of them headed up the stairs with Sumi and Ilya assisting Harakin. They slipped out of the secret entrance behind the old fan cage and started to head inland toward Gate Town.

The city was beginning to lighten with the rising sun.

"That pile of rubble," Ilya said, pointing toward the ruins of the Messiah Tower, "was until recently, the home and headquarters for many of the city's Messiahs. They're the ones who attacked Gate Town a few months back. Good riddance," she added.

"They're still out there," Dozi commented.

"Yeah, but the resistance took out a lot of them, and now they don't have a base."

Harakin asked, "Who are these..." but she groaned and grabbed her neck. Sumi and Ilya stopped walking and held her upright, but Harakin held up her hand to indicate that she was alright. She decided to keep her question brief. "Messiahs?"

Ilya continued. "We told Sumi a little about them already while you rested. They are a group of super-strong people who stole their power by murdering Shifts like us, and eating their mantis glands. They're bad people." She then seemed to correct herself, "But some Messiahs have left their kind. They aren't part of that group anymore, like Auntie Peg."

The quartet reached the edge of Gate Town and Dozi informed their new friends, "This is actually the safest place for Shifts to live, and more specifically farther in, the neighborhood of Shifton."

"Why don't you live there?" Sumi asked Ilya.

She shrugged. "I lived as a human and kept my gifts a secret for so long that it's still easy for me to do."

They took their time with Harakin through the quiet streets, and Ilya pointed out when they entered Shifton.

After a few more blocks, Dozi said, "That's the house, there," and she nodded toward the end of the street.

Ilya knocked on the front door. "They're going to be surprised to see us at such an hour," she commented.

The latch on the other side clicked and Theolan opened the door.

"Well, hello there, ladies," he exclaimed. "To what do we owe this early morning pleasure? And hello, new friends," he added to the two other women who he did not recognize.

"This is Sumi and Harakin," Dozi informed him. "We are hoping your hubby can take a look at the wound on her neck."

"Where are my manners?" Theolan questioned the world at large. "Come in, come in! *Honey*," he called back into the house, "we've got company!"

"Who's here?" Tchama's voice hollered from the kitchen. Her head popped out, and her eyes lit up. "Dozi! Ilya!" Tchama came into the foyer and wrapped each of them in a single-armed embrace. A sash with rainbow stripes was pinned around her neck, and it draped over her recent injury, covering the healed remains of her shoulder.

Ilya stepped close and asked Tchama quietly, "How are you feeling today?"

Tchama guffawed. "You say that as if you don't come to check on me almost every single day." She tried to speak cheerfully, but her tone was a little flat.

Ilya worried that if Tchama stopped trying to keep herself pepped up, she would plummet into the dark dour doldrums of misery.

Sumi came up behind Ilya and Tchama and said, "They told me what happened to you at the battle recently. How has it been, learning to do everything with one hand?"

Tchama sighed. "There are frustrating moments. I've broken a few things here in the house," she added, and she turned a guilty expression toward Theolan.

"You've done so well," he encouraged.

Dozi interrupted. "Theolan, we need your husband!"

"Greetings!" the mystic called from upstairs. The little round man descended and hugged Ilya and Dozi. "Introductions, introductions!"

"This is Sumi," Dozi indicated, "and this is Harakin, who needs some fairly immediate medical attention!"

The mystic snapped to action. "I noticed the bandage but suspected it was an old injury." He was already heading into another part of the house.

"It's very fresh," Dozi informed him as she followed with Harakin.

"To the kitchen," the mystic instructed them all. "Tell me your name again, my dear," he requested of Harakin, and she did. "What happened to you?" he asked.

Harakin looked at Sumi, who replied for her.

"We were on a mission. It didn't go well. I thought she was going to die." Then Sumi added quietly, "I thought she *did* die."

The mystic gingerly removed the bandage from Harakin's neck. "That won't be happening on this day," he informed Sumi with a confident smile. He then looked into Harakin's eyes. "You're not going to die, Harakin. Did I get the pronunciation correct?"

Harakin nodded, but she winced.

The mystic looked mortified. "I apologize for making you move your neck! That was terrible timing on my part. Please, remain still for the sake of your wound," he warned her.

It looked angry, but he treated her with masterful skill.

"I need to put in a few stitches," the mystic said. "This is not going to feel nice, but it will be over quickly." He dabbed some liquid on a cotton ball and pressed it around the edges of the wound. "You're gonna have one serious scar when this heals, but at least it *will* heal."

Harakin was used to the rough treatment of the medics back at the compound, but the mystic's ministrations were nothing like theirs.

He threaded a curved needle and said over his shoulder, "Tchama, can Harakin hold your hand?"

"My *only* hand," she muttered to herself.

The mystic looked at Harakin. "Tchama's very strong, and she can take it, no matter how hard you need to squeeze her fingers."

Tchama sat beside Harakin and extended her arm with a small smile. They clasped hands.

The mystic said, "Here we go," and Harakin sucked air through her teeth as he began to apply the first stitch.

Suddenly, the horrible wound started to glow.

"It's doing it again!" Sumi declared.

The mystic looked shocked. "I can feel it," he said.

"Heat?" Theolan asked.

The mystic furrowed his brow. "No," and he touched the wound with his fingertip, "I can feel something *physical* where the light is."

"That's what she can do," Sumi replied, "make light into knives, but before this, I'd never seen it come from a wound."

The mystic looked into Harakin's eyes. "You can make light become physical?"

"Yes, that's how I survived," she said, looking back at Sumi. "When my throat was cut, I could feel myself getting weaker, and I told my light to stop the bleeding."

They all looked at her glowing neck.

"Then you brought down the entire castle," Sumi whispered.

Everyone turned in Sumi's direction.

She scrunched up her face in concentration. "When I thought Harakin was about to die, she made..." she paused to find the right word, "a ceiling, yeah, it was like a ceiling of her light daggers, and she brought it crashing down on the throne room. I escaped back to the compound without her." Sumi's voice trailed off.

"Castle?" Tchama asked.

Sumi took Harakin's other hand. "You haven't even told me how you survived when the roof caved in."

Harakin moaned, but then she said, "I'm not certain." She took a deep breath. "I told my light to stop the bleeding, but in that instant, I resigned myself to die with all those secondary targets." She sighed. "Everyone else was killed by my assault, but somehow I was protected. It was like a bubble of light appeared on its own and shielded me from my knives."

The mystic touched the solid light on Harakin's neck again. "It seems to be keeping your wound closed, but can you please make it go away for a moment? I know these stitches won't feel good, but you *need* a few of them."

She closed her eyes and the light vanished.

"I'm sorry for the discomfort," the mystic said, as he completed the first stitch.

Harakin squeezed Tchama and Sumi's hands as the mystic continued.

"I think five should do the trick. Then I'll apply some ointment and a bandage that you will be able to remove as necessary." He moved swiftly. "That's two stitches done," he informed her. "Three more..." he said and paused. "Last one."

Harakin was gritting her teeth, but her solid light did not return to the wound.

"Finished!" the mystic proclaimed. "That was the rough part. This will be easier." He smeared a little bright green salve over the stitches, and Harakin let out a sharp breath. The mystic then wrapped her neck in a fresh cloth bandage. "Perfect," he concluded.

"Thank you," Harakin managed. She looked down at Tchama's hand. "Did I hurt you?" she asked.

Tchama gave her a half smile. "No, it's pretty hard to hurt me." She shrugged and her smile faded.

Sumi gingerly pulled her fingers away from Harakin's other hand. "Ouch," she whispered.

Harakin smiled apologetically.

Theolan stepped up to his husband, turned to face their guests, and he offered, "Breakfast?"

The group ate muffins with plenty of butter, and the mystic insisted that Sumi and Harakin stay for the day, so that he could give her a fresh bandage in several hours. He also extended the invitation to Dozi and Ilya, and the group spent the morning together.

As noon approached, Theolan said, "If you lot are staying through lunch, you're in for a treat. Peggy and Dot are coming here today with Ninyani."

As if on cue, the front door opened and Auntie Peg called out in a singsong voice, "*Yoo-hoo!* Anyone home?" She strode in wearing tall high-heeled boots, leggings, and a corset. A bright blue wig was on her head, and her makeup was as dramatic as ever. "Hey, *gurls*," she said to them all, "the queens have arrived!"

Ninyani was behind Auntie Peg. The boy was dressed in a lovely floral frock and a dark skirt. He was draped in a sheer shawl and there was a little turquoise eye shadow on his upper lids. Tchama waved at him and he scampered over to her.

"I love your rainbow scarf!" he proclaimed in a squeaky voice.

A tall woman entered behind the boy. She closed the door and struck a pose. "Who's serving the cuntiest cunt?" she asked, expectantly awaiting an answer.

"Dot," the mystic said to her, "you look as ravishing as always!" The little round man stepped up and took her hand. He kissed the back of it, then turned to the others. "This is Harakin and Sumi," he declared. "They are new friends who will be staying with Dozi and Ilya." He waved his hand toward the three individuals who just arrived. "And this is Ninyani, Dotty Marbles or *Dot*, and the most elegant of women, folks 'round here call her Auntie Peg, but we all have the privilege of referring to her as Peggy," the mystic finished.

"This magical trio lives together not far from here," Theolan added.

"Charmed," Auntie Peg replied with a wide smile, and she reached out to Harakin and Sumi.

Sumi's face scrunched up in confusion. "You're… men?" she asked.

Auntie Peg burst out laughing and Dotty Marbles snickered behind her.

"We are *queens*, my dear," Auntie Peg replied, "but yes," she added with a chuckle, "my beloved, Dotty Marbles, and I undress at night down to the boys that are hidden beneath all this fabulousity and glamor."

Auntie Peg now posed for them all and Ninyani giggled at her display.

"Righty-oh," the mystic said, rubbing his belly, "who's hungry?"✪

Chapter 17 – The First Organic Mechanic of Teshon City

After moving into Gate Town, Olona focused on using her skills to help people. Her days were spent healing the injured, and Olona enjoyed her practice. Some locals were hesitant to accept treatments with the bizarre machines that she used; most were unfamiliar with or at least unsure of the arts performed by organic mechanics.

When Olona and Tisa left their shack in the Spritehood, they moved into the first floor of an empty building that they discovered at the edge of Shifton. Over the next few weeks, Olona's practice grew, and she started treating people in their new home. She and Tisa moved upstairs into the space above, and the ground level became Olona's storefront and care station.

It was not long before the shop was thriving. Weeks turned into months, and her practice became popular across Teshon City. New people came to her daily.

"Welcome to the First Organic Mechanic of Teshon City," Olona called out as a bell rang and a woman opened the front door. "It's our six-month anniversary! What can I do for you?"

"You fixed me neighbor's leg," the woman replied to Olona. She was wearing an eyepatch. "I was just wonderin' if'n you couldn't do something for me eye. It's goin' on me. Can't see nothin' out of it for near a year now." She lifted the patch.

Olona put down the joint she was smoking and asked the woman, "Are you in any pain?"

"Nah," she replied, "there was a dull ache for a while when me vision first started fading, but it don't hurt none."

Olona raised her hands. "May I touch your face?"

The woman nodded and Olona gently felt the space around the orbital socket.

"I can replace your eye with a mechanical one. It's a procedure that is not approved by the organic mechanics guild where I trained," Olona said, and the woman looked nervous, but Olona continued. "I've actually given myself an optical upgrade. I've got my own partially mechanical eye. So, let's see what we can do for you."

During her days, Olona mended injuries, helped people with worn-out joints, and gave strength to folks who had grown weak.

One evening, Tisa came home to find Olona in an excited state.

"Tisa, I met a man from Xin today!" she declared. "He let me copy a map he owned and explained why there are so few people who have ever made the journey from here to there or vice versa. Take a look!"

She pointed at a roll of parchment on the tabletop. "Help me spread this out." Olona's drawing was scratchy, but she started indicating different sections of it. "The man said these mountains that separate Xin from the region around Teshon City are virtually impassible. Also, it's apparently almost impossible to sneak through Gunge." Olona shot Tisa a proud expression. "But *we* did," she added with a smile, and she continued. "He told me there's also some sort of treacherous ocean phenomenon that doesn't let any seafaring vessels travel south of Hazel Cove." Olona indicated a section of the ocean and said, "Whatever's in the water starts below that region and stretches out into the sea. I guess it goes up, encircles Teshon Harbor, and connects to the land far to the north of the city. He didn't know if it was a massive coral reef or some sort of underwater topographical anomaly, but he said that ships can't go between this region and Xin."

"Strange," Tisa said.

"So, because of the mountains and oceanic barrier," Olona continued, pointing at it again, "coupled with Gunge, almost no one's made the journey, and it's only possible on foot. The Oselians must have known some way to deal with whatever is out in the ocean. Maybe their warships smashed it, and it regrew, or maybe whatever it is appeared afterward, I don't know," she concluded.

"Well, I guess that explains that," Tisa replied.

"We did something that very few others have accomplished," Olona said in amazement. She put her arm around Tisa. "We are pretty impressive," she added with a smile. "I wonder what else we are going to achieve."★

Chapter 18 – Confrontation

In the darkness of the night, Tisa walked beside Lahari. They headed away from the hidden hideout of the Biological Shift vigilantes, and the two of them made their way into Gate Town toward Shifton.

"I, for one, am in favor," Lahari said.

"This is what I was *made* for," Tisa replied, "stopping bad people and protecting my own kind."

"I think one or two of the others in the group still need convincing," Lahari stated. "They are resistant to adding new members, and I'll be honest, none of us has even considered adding someone who isn't a Bio-Shift. Tualu surprised us all by bringing you tonight."

"I may not be a Bio-Shift, but I have just as much hatred for those who kill us, as all of you do." Tisa then asked, "Can I talk to you about the way you look?"

Lahari gave her a sideways glance with her yellow eyes and answered in a hesitant tone. "I guess so. Never been around Bio-Shifts?"

Tisa stopped walking.

Lahari paused and turned. "What is it?" she asked.

A sob choked Tisa, and she brought her hands to her face. "Liovia," she managed to say through her shuddering breaths, "I was friends with..." but her voice fell, and Tisa cried.

It took a moment for her to catch her breath and calm down enough to explain. "I used to live with a woman who the locals called a witch. Her skin was not like other peoples', and she had wings, but she couldn't fly."

Lahari waited for Tisa to say more, but she remained silent, and Lahari quietly asked, "You used to live with a Bio-Shift?"

Tisa nodded. "I think so. We didn't have terms for what we are." Her voice broke again as she said, "I mean, what Liovia was. I don't know why she looked so different, but I *did* know that we were the same, even though I look like a human. For more than half my life, I lived with her in the forest near the village where I was born, but the villagers... the villagers..." Tisa's voice failed her again.

"They killed her, didn't they?" Lahari said gently.

Tisa nodded again as fresh tears streamed down her cheeks.

"I'm so sorry," Lahari replied in a gentle tone.

Tisa cuffed her eyes with her shirtsleeve and sniffed hard.

"We're nearly there," Lahari added. "It's just around this corner."

A moment later, the two of them were at her house.

"This is where I live with my dads," Lahari said, as she opened the front door. She stepped back for Tisa to enter and called out, "Hi, dads!"

Quite a few people were already in the small interior of their home.

"Lahari!" Theolan replied in delight, but Harakin let out a bloodcurdling scream and leapt up from her seat.

Sumi was beside her and slipped from her chair to the floor.

Ninyani and Tchama both jumped and he wrapped his little arms around her.

"Oh, no, no, no!" the mystic quickly interjected with a friendly chuckle. "Harakin, that's Lahari. She's my daughter. We told you about her."

"*You!*" Harakin shrieked. Flashes of light materialized in the air, and her devastating blades flew through the crowded room toward the two women entering the house.

Auntie Peg and Dotty Marbles grabbed Ilya and Dozi, and the queens pulled them back from the line of fire.

"What the…" Lahari started to say, but Tisa's powers reacted by reflex.

A void disc appeared in a flash of darkness and a serpentine creature protruded from it. Tentacles extended from its body, and each of Harakin's daggers of light was snatched and disappeared into Tisa's shadow opening.

"No!" Harakin raged.

Sumi jumped up from the floor. "Harakin, what are you doing?!" she yelled, as Harakin launched a barrage of solidified light beams at Tisa.

A massive hole opened in the space between them and it manifested a bushy plant of blackness that absorbed the light.

"What is happening?!" the mystic yelled to the room at large.

"Please, stop this!" Ninyani cried.

Theolan held his husband close, and the mystic asked his daughter, "Lahari, are you consuming these energies? *What is going on here?*"

"I'll kill you!" Harakin wailed at Tisa, and she put every ounce of her energy into her assault.

Another void of darkness appeared, but Sumi cried, *"Stop!"* and she opened one of her doorways between Tisa and Harakin.

In an instant, everything ceased.

The light was gone.

The shadows were gone.

Sumi's doorway was gone.

"Harakin, what's wrong?!" Sumi asked, grabbing her hands. "Why are you attacking them?"

"That woman!" Harakin paused and stared at Tisa. "That's… that's…" she stuttered.

"Who is that? Do you know her?" Sumi asked. "I've never seen her before in my life!"

Harakin's eyes were locked on Tisa's and she spoke in a frightened voice. "I thought… I thought she was one of the officers from the compound."

"She's not," Sumi replied emphatically. "Look at her! We've never seen her before! She is not whoever you think she is."

"You're safe here with all of us!" Ilya added, trying to reassure Harakin.

Sumi turned and stared at Tisa. "How did you do that?"

Tisa looked at Lahari.

Lahari cleared her throat and said, "This is Tisa. She's a Shift, and a new friend."

Even after the chaos, Tisa felt Lahari's word *friend* deep in her soul.

Then Sumi interrupted in a hushed tone. *"What are you?"* She looked astonished.

Lahari turned to her father.

"This is my daughter," the mystic declared, "We were telling you about her. Her name is Lahari." He stepped up and embraced her.

She said to him, "It's crowded in here."

The mystic, Theolan, Tchama, Dozi, Ilya, Sumi, Auntie Peg, Dotty Marbles, and Ninyani were all relieved that the violence was at an end, and they made room for the other two arrivals. Introductions were made with everyone, and the group started chatting.

Harakin tentatively sidled toward Tisa. "I'm sorry," she said quietly. "I didn't… I wasn't…" She was uncertain what to say. "I thought you… I don't know… it's not…"

"Hey," Tisa said calmly, "it's okay. I don't know who you thought I was, but it wasn't me."

"No," Harakin confirmed in a tone that sounded more miserable with every word, "you're not who I was afraid you were. I'm... I'm sorry," she concluded, on the verge of tears.

Tisa reached out and took the teenager's hand. "We are like one another, you and I. You're like me, and I'm like you. We're Shifts, and in my time in Teshon City, I've learned that Shifts protect their own kind." She squeezed Harakin's hand. "Me and you, we're on the same side."

Theolan stood. "Well, I need a cuppa. Who else wants one?" He headed into the kitchen and set the kettle to boil.

His husband stepped up to Tisa, and Harakin headed over to Sumi with an embarrassed frown. The two of them started whispering together.

The mystic gave Tisa a curious look and asked, "What were those things?"

"I can make shadows," she said, and she conjured a disc that was like a hole punched out of reality. One of her small helper forms rose from it and waved.

"It's so cute!" Ninyani squealed with delight.

He reached out to touch it, and the little round shadow creature jumped from the disc and landed on his wrist. It ran up Ninyani's arm to his shoulder and he giggled with delight. The thing hopped over his head, ran down his opposite arm, then leapt back into the disk and disappeared.

Ninyani was beaming, and Tisa could not help but smile.

"Anyone else feeling as lucky as I am?" the mystic asked everyone. "Three new friends all in one day, wow!" He beamed at the group. "So, Tisa, you said you're only been in Teshon City for a year or so. Did you grow up in one of the nearby villages?"

She shook her head. "Oh, no, I didn't. I'm from Xin, the lands to the far south, a town called Kestapoli."

The mystic looked astonished. "*Really?* How is it possible we met the three of you all on the same day, and that you're from a place none of us have ever heard of before? What are the chances?" he mused.

Tisa turned to Harakin and Sumi in amazement. "You're from Xin, too?"

"That's where the compound is," Sumi confirmed.

"How did you two get here? It took my partner and I something like two and a half months of hiking through the mountains to make it all the way to this region."

Sumi looked at Dozi and Ilya, and she replied to Tisa, "We needed a safe place. I opened a doorway and it led us into their home. They helped Harakin with her neck injury, fed us, and then brought us here this morning so he could treat her." Sumi nodded to the mystic.

"That's fresh?" Tisa asked Harakin, and she placed her hand on her own neck, indicating Harakin's bandage. "Are you okay?"

Harakin looked sheepish. "I'm alright," she replied quietly. "I'm... I'm sorry," she said again in a whisper.

"It's okay," Tisa reassured her. "You don't need to worry anymore. Can you tell me, why did you two leave Xin?"

Sumi and Harakin made eye contact, but Dozi spoke up and said, "They were prisoners, and they were made to do terrible things."

"And they don't ever have to go back," added Ilya.

"That's right!" Theolan concurred. "Incidentally," he added turning to Tisa, "what made *you* leave?"

She looked at the group and asked, "Are you familiar with the monsters of Gunge?"

Not a single one of them knew what Tisa was talking about.

"There's a region in the northeast of Xin," she informed them, "where creatures live who used to be human." She went on to explain how the monsters hunted from time to time, and how Liovia could see it happening in advance, giving them the opportunity to flee. Tisa told the group of Liovia's death, about meeting Olona, and their long journey to Teshon City.

"Liovia was a Bio-Shift," Lahari informed her father, and the mystic looked at Tisa with compassion in his eyes.

"I'm so sorry for your loss. We're happy you're here. And I, for one, can't wait to meet Olona," he added.

Tisa's eyes kept moving back to her fellow Xinitians. She was curious about them.

The large group stayed together late into the night, talking about the places they were from, and sharing some of their past experiences. When everyone finally decided to call it a night, they all started to leave, but Dozi came up with an idea.

She asked Sumi, "Can you make another one of your doorways that opens in my basement so that all four of us could just walk through, like you've talked about?"

Sumi paused and looked at her. "I didn't even know I could bring someone with me until that last mission. I don't know." She closed her eyes, reached out with her powers, and she felt for the basement. It came to her instantly and she opened her eyes. "It's there," Sumi said. She took Harakin's hand. "I think we all need to be connected."

Dozi and Ilya both held onto Sumi's other hand, and there was a blink, then the four of them were standing together in Dozi's basement.

"Wow," Ilya whispered.

"It worked," marveled Sumi.

Dozi felt woozy. "I didn't like that at all," she said in a quavering voice. "I think I'll just walk home next time."✪

Chapter 19 – Lahari, S'Kay, Gawa, & Ijeron

"No," argued S'Kay, "I don't want to add anyone new, especially someone who's not a Bio-Shift." She ruffled the feather-like protrusions all over her body.

"Tualu chose Tisa, just like he chose Lahari," Gawa retorted, and the marblesque patterns on her skin shifted with an excited energy.

"Why does his opinion count for so much?" S'Kay asked.

"Listen," Lahari interjected, "he is just as key to what we are doing as the rest of us, and since he doesn't talk, the rare times that he does communicate with us are important. I don't know why he brought us a Shift who looks like a human, as opposed to another Bio-Shift, but maybe there's a reason."

Lahari continued. "Tisa is also older than all of us, so maybe that has something to do with it. Ijeron, you have a new target that you'd like to present. Tell us about it." She waved for a young man with skin like liquid mercury to step up and share his information.

"*Why?*" S'Kay barked before Ijeron could say a word. "Why do we need someone old and normal-looking?"

Gawa was annoyed. "What's your problem, S'Kay?"

The bird-woman replied flatly, "I don't like humans."

"*Tisa's not a human!*" Lahari implored. "She's a Shift, and that means she can do something; she has some power that can kill Messiahs, just like each of us. She told us about that pack of hunters she slaughtered, and I've already shared with you all about the Bio-Shift who Tisa used to live with. I think few people could be as sympathetic to us and our cause."

Gawa asked S'Kay, "Why are you so opposed to letting Tisa join us? What's the harm in adding someone, especially now? We've slain so many Messiahs in this city that we've disrupted their stranglehold on the population." She looked around at the others. "The Messiahs still don't know who we are, as far as we know, and we've become a force to be reckoned with. Diversification can only make us stronger."

"I don't trust anyone normal-looking," S'Kay responded. "She can't possibly know what it's like to be one of our kind. I worry that she might expose us."

"You mean *betray us*, right?" Ijeron asked, finally adding his thoughts to the discussion. "You inherently think she's an enemy, just because she's not a Bio-Shift, but who would she betray or expose us to? It's not like she's in cahoots with the Messiahs or Demifea; at the very least, she's one of our allies."

"I just mean that if we are going to be taking on different types of missions," S'Kay explained, "I worry that something will go wrong, and it will affect all of us. Our stealth attacks on the different groups of Messiahs around the city have been an overwhelming success. I guess I'm just worried about change and what it will bring."

S'Kay sighed and continued. "I guess I'm always going to be resistant to adding new members. You all had to convince me about Yxida and Khano." She turned to the young man with skin like metal. "And even you, Ijeron. I'm sorry," she added, "but anyway, tell us about the next potential target you've found."

Gawa interjected, "Don't you see the benefit of adding different people to what we're doing?"

"I understand," S'Kay replied. "It just feels weird, and I don't like it." She crossed her arms and furrowed her feathered brow.

"Go ahead, Ijeron," Lahari said.

He began sharing his information. "A contingent of Messiahs has fled the city and taken up residence to the south in the Lesser Lighthouse. The report I heard from Brokenpointe stated that a large family was in charge of maintaining the light, but they were all murdered. The Messiahs have set up some sort of barricade blocking access to the minor peninsula where the lighthouse sits."

"What do we need a non-Bio-Shift for?" S'Kay asked in an irritated voice.

Gawa huffed. "We don't know yet."

"Yeah, and there are a lot of Messiahs holed up in the lighthouse," Ijeron added.

"I stayed in Brokenpointe once," Lahari reminisced. Then she added, "Killed some people while I was there."

The others looked at her.

She looked right back at them with her yellow eyes.

For a moment, no one spoke.

"You're not going to tell us any more about that?" Gawa asked.

"I don't need to explain my past, and it doesn't pertain to Ijeron's mission. Suffice it to say, they were not good people. What else do we know about the lighthouse?"

"The locals have abandoned the area," Ijeron continued. "No one from Brokenpointe will approach the barricade."

"You know I'm game," Gawa said. "When do we take them out? Do we know how many there are?"

"The lighthouse is not very large," Lahari stated. "I would guess no more than 20 Messiahs."

Ijeron countered, "My contact said the family that the Messiahs slaughtered was big, five parents and twelve kids. The lighthouse might be bigger inside than it looks, and because of the possibility of many enemies inside it, I don't think it's a good idea to have Tualu teleport us into the building. I also predict an unlikelihood of success by using stealth," he added. "They are patrolling the peninsula and will certainly know we're coming. We should expect heavy resistance."

"It is necessary that they die," Lahari stated, "and we're going to need the whole team." She ran her fingers over the black quills on the sides of her face. "How soon can we do it?"

Gawa said, "Khano and Yxida were essential the last time we brought them. They were also enthusiastic about the next time we would need them. I'll let them know, and I'll tell Tualu."

Lahari added, "I think we should clear out the lighthouse tomorrow night."

"So, what's the plan exactly?" S'Kay asked. "If we can't sneak up on the lighthouse, and we think it's too dangerous for Tualu to bring us straight inside it, how are we supposed to take them out?" She was still hesitant in regard to Tisa joining, but she was united with them all in her feelings about Messiahs.

"Can Tualu bring us to the forest outside of Brokenpointe, and then we can approach the lighthouse from the mainland?" Gawa asked.

Ijeron looked around at the others. "That seems like our only option."

Less than 24 hours later, the team of six Biological Shifts was gathered in their hidden underground space. Lahari, S'Kay, Gawa, Ijeron, Khano, and Yxida were ready for battle.

Lahari's spines were extended, and she looked ominous.

The patterns on Gawa's skin seemed to be radiating from her heartspace.

S'Kay's feathers rippled as in a breeze.

Ijeron was standing still in anticipation, and his mirrored skin reflected everyone else's movements. This was only his third mission, and he was anxious.

Khano was huge. He towered over the others. His appearance was similar to a bear. Like the group's fallen companion, Eroli, Khano's entire body was covered in thick hair, but his was so dark brown that it was almost black. His eyes were similar to Gawa's, with no pupils or irises, and they glowed with blue light.

Yxida was the newest recruit to the vigilante group, and their last attack was her first time out with the other Biological Shifts. She was an individual of short stature, standing about four feet tall. She possessed tusks like a boar, very long pointed ears that stood higher than the top of her head, and a pair of curved horns that grew around her unusual ears. The photonova gland in her brain provided her with the ability to manipulate the molecular structure of objects.

The group waited.

Minutes slowly ticked by in tense silence.

"Where is Tualu?" Lahari asked. "Gawa, you told him about tonight, right?"

"Of course, I did," she replied. "I don't know where he could be. Since he doesn't talk, he didn't indicate to me that he *wasn't* going to be joining us. He didn't give me any kind of sign at all."

"Without Tualu, we can't even get close," Ijeron said. "Is it possible he doesn't want us to do this?"

S'Kay scoffed. "We decided on tonight. What does he know that we don't?"

"Maybe it's not about what he knows," Gawa retorted. "Maybe it's something else."

The six of them grumbled together as the minutes ticked by, and after more than an hour of waiting, they gave up on Tualu. The pre-violence anticipation and tension had slowly dissipated with the lack of activity, and under the cover of darkness, the group decided to head back into the city.

"I'm going to Red Raven's," Lahari informed the others. "You're all welcome to join me, if you'd like."

A few minutes later, they entered the pub, and the group took a seat at a booth in the corner. The place was not crowded, and only a few patrons were seated at the bar.

Then Tualu materialized right next to Gawa.

"*Where were you?*" S'Kay snapped at him. "I know, I know," she said before anyone could interject. "I know you're not going to say anything."

Tualu's rectangular mechanical form, without limbs or a head, gave S'Kay no reply.

"Order a round for everyone," Lahari said to Gawa. "Tonight's not the night."★

Chapter 20 – Found Family

"Olona!" Tisa cried with delight, as she opened the front door to the shop and headed up the stairs to their living quarters. "I met this great group of people!"

"What, really?" Olona replied. "That's wonderful! I'm so happy that you've found some folks to call friends!"

"Will you come meet them?" Tisa asked with a beaming smile.

"Oh, I don't need to be friends with your new friends," Olona replied.

Tisa's expression dropped. "Why don't you want to meet the people I've met? Making friends has been so hard for me. I could really use your support."

"I do support you, Tisa," Olona said with a smile, "but I've got lots of friends, and I don't want to interfere with your life."

"But you're a major part of my life," Tisa retorted. "We live together. What if I have them over here someday? Will they just be perfect strangers to you?"

"No," Olona said with a chuckle, "they'll be *your* friends, and I will look forward to meeting them then."

"Why are you being like this?"

Olona paused. "I'm not being like anything," she said. "I just don't need more friends."

"How can you say that? Everyone needs friends!"

Olona put her hands up in a placating gesture. "Tisa, I don't even know what we're arguing about. I want you to make friends, and I know it's been difficult, so I'm happy that you've..."

"I just want you to meet them," Tisa pouted, "because I know they'll love you."

"I love it when you act like *you're* the bratty 19 year old," Olona teased.

Tisa scoffed. "I'm not bratty!"

"No," Olona laughed, "I was saying that *I'm* bratty, and you're being like me, even though you're over 30."

"Why won't you meet them?" Tisa whined.

"Okay, okay, I'll meet them," Olona agreed. "I wasn't trying to be difficult," she added under her breath. "Will you tell me a little about them?"

"Several are Bio-Shifts."

Olona perked up at the mention of the rarely-seen but incredibly unique individuals who made up the small percentage of the population that were Biological Shifts. Since the underground became unlivable more than a year earlier, many of them now dwelt in Gate Town, and particularly Shifton, and Olona was always fascinated by them.

"You made friends with a bunch of Bio-Shifts?" Olona asked in excitement. "How did that happen? Where did you meet them?"

Tisa furrowed her brow. "I'm not sure exactly how it all happened. I was here earlier, and…" she hesitated. "I think he was a Bio-Shift, but he looked like a big machine. The others called him Tualu. While I was here, he appeared."

"Appeared?"

"Yeah," Tisa confirmed, "out of thin air. There was a hand-shaped symbol on him, and I touched it. I can't explain it, but there was something comforting about his presence, like I trusted him." Tisa smiled. "I think he teleported us, because suddenly I was in an underground chamber, and there were a bunch of Bio-Shifts!"

Olona looked amazed. "You should have opened with that," she teased in a tone of playful sarcasm. *"Hey, Olona,"* Olona said in a dramatic impression of Tisa's voice, *"I met a bunch of Bio-Shifts today."*

Tisa snorted a laugh and slapped at Olona. "Shut your face! I don't sound like that!" she laughed. "Anyway, they told me about their team, and I told them about when I got attacked last year."

"Their team? Tell me about that," Olona asked.

"They didn't tell me much. I know that they've hunted some Messiahs, and they were somehow involved with the battle of Gate Town a few months ago," Tisa explained. "They wanted to discuss things amongst themselves before they told me anything more."

"Do you think they want you to join them?"

"They seemed to think Tualu wanted me to be part of the team, which is why he teleported me to them, but he can't speak, so they wanted to talk about it."

Olona was enthralled. "Wow," she said.

"Lahari, that's the name of the one who seems to be in charge. She's got blue skin and these black spines all over her." Tisa's eyes were sparkling. "There was a woman whose skin moved with pretty patterns, kind of like what an oil slick on water looks like.

Another woman, who I think had feathers all over her, she didn't talk much. They told me there were a few others from their group who weren't there."

"How many?" asked Olona.

"They didn't say. When we all left, Lahari took me to her house where she lives with her dads. There was a whole bunch of people there, like a party or something. That's where I met everyone. Oh," Tisa paused, "and one of them attacked me, another Shift girl. She's probably close to your age."

"Wait, wait, wait," Olona interrupted, "one of them attacked you?!"

Tisa shrugged. "Apparently she thought I was someone from her past." She then looked like she forgot something. "Oh, and she and another girl are from Xin!"

"What?" Olona asked in surprise. "You met someone else from Xin?"

"Two people!"

"And one of them attacked you?"

"Yes," Tisa confirmed, "she can create knives out of light, but my shadows were able to protect me. It was intense for a minute. Then the other girl from Xin, who is also a Shift, she used her power and something happened." Tisa furrowed her brow. "It was like all three of our powers negated and canceled each other out. It was really weird."

Olona looked curious.

Tisa continued and told Olona about the others in the group, although in the moment, she realized that she could not remember most of their names. She did her best to describe each person.

"Now will you come meet them?" Tisa eventually asked.

"Of course," Olona replied with an apologetic smile, "I'd love to meet them."✪

Chapter 21 – The Gathering

"Where's Tisa?" Harakin whined. The strange connection between their powers fascinated her, and she was quite taken with Tisa.

"I'm sure she'll be along shortly," the mystic said in a cheery voice. "Besides, I'm not finished cooking yet. I'd much prefer that she and her friend arrive when the food's close to ready."

"I wonder what she's like," Harakin said in a wistful tone. "I mean, the other girl from Xin."

"*Knock, knock!*" Auntie Peg called from the front door of the mystic's house. She added a singsongy, "We're here!" She was in a flowing dress and stylish jacket. Her wig was black with red and white stripes running through it, and her makeup was vibrant shades of red and silver.

"Tisa?!" Harakin called out.

"No, sorry, dear," Dotty Marbles replied. "It's just little ol' us." Her makeup was in shades of purple and she donned a matching wig. Her pink poodle skirt was polka dotted in yet more hues of vivid violet. "If she's not here yet, I'm sure she'll be along shortly. We brought dessert!" Dotty Marbles added. She held up a pastry box.

"What a coincidence," Theolan said as he came down from upstairs, "Lahari and I also picked up some dessert for today."

"I'm not mad that there's extra dessert," the mystic cooed at them.

Sumi and Lahari came in from the back garden with a basket of fresh herbs that they harvested from a tiny garden box.

"Those are beautiful, daughter!" the mystic proclaimed. He kissed Lahari on her spiny blue-skinned cheek.

She grinned and her yellow eyes sparkled at him.

Ninyani came in behind the two queens. "Where's Tchama?" he asked the group at large. He was wearing a spaghetti strap tank top with a robin's-egg blue cardigan over it and a pleated tartan skirt. His hair was coifed up and he was sparkling with a little glittery lip shimmer and blush.

Tchama's voice came from upstairs. "I'll be down in a minute! You can come up if you want!"

Ninyani knew she was talking to him, and he skipped up the stairs to find her.

"There's not enough room for all of us at the table," the mystic said to his husband, "so let's set it with as many plates as we can fit, and we'll put a few place settings here on the counter. Or if anyone would like to sit over in the lounging chairs that will work also."

There was another knock at the door.

"Tisa?" Harakin said again hopefully. She opened the front door, and sure enough, it was Tisa.

"Hi, everyone," Tisa said in a more timid voice than she intended. "This is Olona." Tisa stepped aside and Olona entered behind her.

"Welcome to our home!" Theolan declared. "You are most welcome here and we are so thrilled to meet you. Won't you come in and make yourselves at home?"

"That's very kind of you," Olona replied.

Harakin took Tisa's hand. "I'm so glad you came back." There was an awkward pause where Harakin did not know what else to say.

Tisa blushed and responded, "Oh, erm, thanks."

Then Harakin turned and focused on Olona. "You're not old."

Tisa scoffed and playfully smacked the back of Harakin's hand. "Are you saying I am?"

"What? No!" Harakin blurted out. "But, you know, she's like my age," she added with a shrug.

"Yes, indeed, I am 19. My name is Olona, and I come from the land of Xin. Are you one of the others Tisa told me about who are also from the south?"

"Yeah," Harakin replied, "me and Sumi both are." She turned back and Sumi gave Olona a little wave.

"Hello!" Olona said with a smile. Then she saw Lahari and her eyes widened. "You must be," and she looked at Tisa for confirmation, "Lahari?"

Tisa nodded.

"How'd you guess?" Lahari asked. She caused her quills to ripple across her skin in mesmerizing patterns.

"Wow," Olona said, "you're incredible!"

"That she is," her father said. He stepped up to Olona and added, "You can just call me *mystic*," and he wrapped his arms around her in a warm embrace.

Olona laughed out loud and hugged him back. She looked at Tisa again. "You were right," she conceded. "I already very much like this group of friends that you've made."

Dozi and Ilya introduced themselves to Olona, and then Theolan spoke to the entire group.

"Please, come into the kitchen," he urged. "Let's seat ourselves and have some of this lovely meal that my gracious husband has prepared for all of us."

Ninyani and Tchama descended and joined the group.

They all chatted and laughed, asking and answering questions of each other. Tisa and Olona even shared a classic Xinetian song with the group before the mystic broke out dessert.

Lahari and Theolan began to clear the plates as pastries were distributed.

Olona hopped up from her seat and planted herself in the one next to Harakin. "Tisa tells me you can manipulate light. Is it possible for you to show me?" she asked.

"Yeah, okay," Harakin confirmed, "I can make knives from light."

"Is it safe for you to demonstrate?" Olona asked. "I've become pretty familiar with Tisa's shadow energy in the time that we've known each other. It sounds to me like your light powers might be related to her shadows. She can make her shadow disks appear and hover in midair," Olona continued. "Can you do the same thing with your light?"

"Like this?" Harakin asked in reply, and she held up her hand. A blade blinked into existence and floated above her fingertips. It glowed, but the light was not intense.

"Can I touch it? Will it hurt me?" she asked.

Harakin looked over at Sumi and said, "I don't know."

Sumi offered nothing but a shrug.

Olona picked up a spoon from the table with everyone watching her, and she poked the light dagger with it. The spoon made contact with the blade, but nothing happened; there was no reaction, and Olona chanced to touch it. She brought her fingertip to the blade.

"It's solid!" she said, and she looked into Harakin's eyes. "This is amazing!"

Harakin blushed. "Thanks," she mumbled. Her dagger disappeared.

Olona turned to Sumi. "And you can do something, also, right? You're a Shift, too?"

"Yes, I am. I can make doorways that lead from where I am into other places."

Olona furrowed her brow. "Is it a form of teleportation?"

Sumi looked around at the others in the room, but only a few of them had ever seen her power in action. "I guess so," she replied.

"Fascinating," Olona said, "and when Harakin," she paused and looked at her fellow teenager without a hint of judgment, "when you attacked Tisa, then Sumi, you did something and it stopped their fight?" she asked.

Sumi looked uncertain. "I don't know. I opened one of my doorways to try and take away their energies, and I guess that's what happened."

"This is all so interesting," Olona declared. She then looked over at Tchama, who was seated between Dozi and Ilya. "And you've been enhanced, is that correct?"

Tchama fiddled with the beige and burgundy scarf that was draped over her scarred shoulder. "Yes," she said, and she then quickly added, "but I'm not a messiah and I don't want to be called one," and she frowned.

Ilya put her arm around Tchama.

Olona shook her head with a kind smile. "I won't call you that. We don't even use that term where we're from down in Xin. I'm curious about what changed for you. I'd love to test how strong you are now."

"How strong my *one* arm is," Tchama replied in a cynical tone.

"Yes," Olona responded, "I'm sorry you lost your arm, but Tisa told me that your remaining arm is so much stronger now. Would you allow me to test the increase to your strength?"

Tchama looked taken aback. "You're serious?" she asked. "Why do you want to do that?"

Olona made an uncertain expression. "I guess I'm just curious. I've never met anyone like you, or Auntie Peg," and she added, "and I think that I comprehend how different both of your empowerments happened. Really, I only want to see what you can do, if you're comfortable with that," she concluded.

"I don't know," Tchama replied. "How would you do it?"

"Well," Olona said, digging in her bag, "let me fashion a pressure gauge and we can test the strength of some of the muscles in your arm. Is that okay with you?"

Auntie Peg was paying close attention. She seemed very interested in the information that Olona was hoping to determine.

Ilya also seemed very supportive.

Tchama looked around at the others. "I guess so," she said, turning back to Olona.

The group ate their pastries while Olona worked, and before they were finished with their sweets, she said, "Almost done." Then she held out her hand with a strange mechanical device.

"Tchama, just start by squeezing that in your hand," Olona instructed. "It'll register and track the pressure you can exert. I've already calibrated it to my normal hand's squeezing pressure."

Olona placed it in Tchama's palm.

"Okay," Tchama said. She gave the contraption an uncertain look, closed her fist, and crushed it.

"Oh, wow!" Olona said in delighted surprise before Tchama could apologize. "You're exceptionally strong!" She started assembling another device.

"How much stuff do you have in that bag?" Dozi asked.

Olona looked up and around at the group, a little guilty. "I'm sorry," she said. "I've got a tendency to completely take over conversations. Sorry about that." She turned towards Tisa, but Olona was surprised to see that she was beaming at her.

"Well, *I*," Auntie Peg said, "am very much enjoying watching you buzz around us like a busy bumble bee." She chuckled.

Tisa answered Dozi's question. "Olona always has a bag *full* of gear."

Olona grinned. Then she looked at Tchama and said, "This one will be much sturdier." Olona gave the second device a squeeze to calibrate it, and she extended it to Tchama. "Let's try that again," she said in a positive tone.

Tchama's brow furrowed, as she took the device and squeezed. She did not break it this time. Then she opened her hand and extended it to Olona.

"Thank you!" she said. To everyone's surprise, Olona rolled up her sleeve and removed a rectangle of skin from her forearm that turned out to be a false covering. It protected and concealed a device that was held within her flesh. Olona pulled a small silver cable that uncoiled, and she attached it to the device in Tchama's hand.

There was a pause.

Olona chuckled to herself, shook her head, and told the group, "Her strength is literally off the scale that I've been able to program. Tchama, you didn't destroy my second device," Olona explained, "but it came back with an error message, and I don't have the proper equipment to make a gauge that will register your strength. Wow," she whispered again. "That's really impressive."

Tchama was again caught off guard by Olona's complementary words and tone. It was not that everyone with whom she was now friends was not kind or sweet, but this quirky new individual was the first person to display awe and wonder at her change, a change that Tchama spent the past several months *resenting* in her mind. There were moments of frustration where Tchama considered that it would have been better for her to have died on that grimy street during the battle of Gate Town. Olona made Tchama feel, for the first time, like consuming the photonova gland was in fact the right decision.

"How do you not know about Messiahs down in, what is it, Zin?" Thcama asked Olona.

"Xin," she corrected with a smile. "I don't think we have them down there, at least, I've never heard of Messiahs before, but Xinitians also act like Shifts don't exist. We don't even have a word for them that isn't derogatory," Olona continued. "Shifts aren't really talked about; their whole existence is just sort of ignored. I think everyone knows that there's a group of weird..." She caught herself and threw her hands over her mouth. "I'm sorry! That's not what I meant!" she backtracked. "Not *weird*, just, people who can do something different from everyone else, it's not a subject that is discussed."

Tisa said, "I don't think most people in Xin know that it's possible to become a Messiah."

"I have my doubts," Auntie Peg commented, "that there are *no* Messiahs in Xin. I suspect there are little fringe groups, people who have become Messiahs and now congregate together or use their strength to take advantage of people."

"You know, now that you mention it," Olona replied, "the commander of the Tuilii la Ru city guard is exceptionally strong, but I never really thought much about it. I have no idea what made her so strong."

Olona turned back to Tchama, who fidgeted with the sash that hid the stump of her shoulder. "Also, I know that you're not one of them. I'm just curious about your enhancement, so if you're willing, I'd love for you to come to my shop sometime so I can get proper readings on your incredible strength."

Tchama agreed as the final dirty dishes from everyone's dessert were collected, and the large group split up. Dozi, Lahari, and Sumi went outside into the back garden and Olona asked if she could join them. Tisa and Harakin headed with the queens into the sitting room with Ninyani, Tchama, and Ilya. The groups chatted and mingled, switching members, as conversations merged. Olona shared more than one of her joints with the others, and the large group stayed together laughing and talking until almost midnight.

When they were all finally ready to head out, Dotty Marbles made a request of the group. "If any of you are available tomorrow, please feel free to join me in Gate Town. I've been helping to orchestrate repairs from the battle a few months ago. We've done a lot, but there's much more to be done, and we can always use extra hands." She turned to her partner. "Peggy and Ninyani will be at the clinic as usual, but whoever else is available would be greatly appreciated."★

Chapter 22 – Tchama

"Good morning, everyone!" Dotty Marbles called out to the crowd of gathered volunteers. "Thank you so much to all the returning workers, and to the new people who are here today," she added, looking over at the four young women, "welcome."

Dozi, Ilya, Tchama, and Sumi were standing together. Harakin stayed at the mystic's house with him during the day so he could give her wound fresh treatments every few hours.

"Today," Dotty Marbles continued, "we'll be whitewashing the side of a building at the edge of Gate Town. It's already been scrubbed, but it needs to be prepped for a fresh mural."

"What happened to the wall?" whispered Sumi.

"When the Messiahs attacked a few months ago," Ilya replied quietly behind her hand, as Dotty Marbles continued giving instructions, "they set fire to a lot of buildings. Some of them burned down completely, others became structurally unsound. During the battle, lots of Shifts used their energies against the Messiahs, and some of that caused more damage. I don't know exactly what happened to the building, but we should be grateful for today's work; whitewashing is pretty easy. Today looks like it'll be a breeze," she finished with a smile.

"Please, be aware, everyone," Dotty Marbles warned, as she began to lead the group toward their destination, "the structure adjacent to the one we'll be working on is severely damaged, and we do not have the means to repair it. Eventually, it is going to collapse," she stated definitively. "It's marked with warning signs, but I just wanted to remind you all to keep clear of it. Almost there, everyone!"

A moment later, they arrived. Equipment was already waiting for them, and the volunteers worked under Dotty Marbles' directions. The progress was slow and tedious, but there was a jovial atmosphere. People sang songs and children played in the street.

Tchama initially sulked off to the side, doubting that she would be any help with only one arm, but her new enhancement allowed her to join a couple of *very* muscular volunteers. She spent the morning with them, removing a huge pile of fallen masonry away from the wall where the mural was going to go. Tchama's display of strength drew the attention of quite a few amused children.

They marveled as she gripped giant chunks of broken concrete in her single hand and lifted them like they were no more than pebbles. The kids cackled and jeered at the burly men, who needed to work together to lift individual blocks of stone that were not nearly as big as what Tchama could lift by herself.

One little girl was particularly taken and unabashedly stared at Tchama with a look of awe on her face.

In the middle of the day, a group of men showed up with a large pot of stew to feed the volunteers, and everyone was very grateful to them.

Tchama found a seat in the shade, and the enamored little girl came and sat beside her. She did not speak; she simply gawked in adoration.

The work continued through the afternoon and into the evening, and as the sun started to set over the jagged inland mountains, Dotty Marbles called out to the helpers.

"Gather 'round, everyone!"

There was a moment of hubbub as the tired crew huddled near her.

Once Tchama was standing still, the little girl turned up again. She leaned against Tchama's recently-injured side, and Tchama looked down at her. The child reached up and stroked the sash that was pinned over the healed remnant of her shoulder. The scarf she selected that morning was green with a gold ivy pattern, although it was a bit dirty from the day's work.

Dotty Marbles continued. "I just want to take a moment to thank all of you before we head home for the evening. What we're doing here is important. Our repairs of Gate Town over the past few months have bolstered the residents, and it's made a statement to any would-be enemies that we take care of our own." She looked tired, but she was beaming at her helpers. "You are good people, one and all. Thank you again to the UHBS and everyone else who joined us. You're more than welcome to come back tomorrow if you're free, but what you've all done, even just today, has already changed people's lives. Thank you, again. So, if there's nothing else?" Dotty Marbles looked at the other leaders in attendance. "No?" she confirmed. "Very well, thank you, everyone. Have a restful…"

A horrible snap overhead interrupted her.

"*Look out!*" someone screamed.

The nearby building with caution signs around it creaked, and a chunk of the concrete wall dislodged from an upper story. It came hurdling toward the street, as people dove in different directions.

The little girl beside Tchama was frozen, with her eyes locked on the falling stone, but Tchama wrapped her single arm around the child and hunched over her. People cried out, as the old piece of Oselian construction smashed into Tchama's back and shoulders.

Dust and rubble distorted everyone's view for a moment, but when it settled, Tchama was still standing, and the girl was unharmed.

A woman wailed in joy. She ran over and grabbed the child.

"Thank you! Thank you," she cried, squeezing the girl and looking up at Tchama with tears in her eyes. "You saved my daughter!"

Tchama felt dazed, not from being hit by the wall, but by her own thoughts.

"I need to go, Dot," she said quietly to Dotty Marbles, who rushed over to check on her.

"That can't have hurt you, not now that you're like Peggy." She knew how Tchama felt about her newly empowered, albeit one-armed body, and she repeated the mother, "You saved that little girl."

The woman was clutching her child tight and both of them were sobbing.

"I just need to go," Tchama repeated.

"Okay, honey," conceded Dotty Marbles. "We're all getting ready to leave, too. Are you okay?"

"Yeah, Dot, I'm okay, just a little…" she did not finish her thought.

Dotty Marbles looked concerned. "I'm glad you're still with us, and that mother is *very* happy that you just happened to be who you are."

Tchama nodded, turned, and headed down an alley of Gate Town. She wandered aimlessly for a while, until something from the day before drifted into her mind. She turned onto a street that led to the border of Shifton, and she began looking for the sign. Tchama did not remember exactly where it was, but she had passed the storefront on several occasions in recent months, and she knew its general location. Sure enough, a few minutes later, she found it✪

Chapter 23 – The Blood Corruption Clinic

"Please, Auntie Peg," an old man wheezed to her from his cot, "let Ninyani finish reading the chapter." He coughed and Auntie Peg handed him his glass of water.

"Of course, Ninyani can finish reading the chapter," she replied with a smile.

Auntie Peg headed into the hallway and checked several charts as she continued her rounds. The night shift was about to start, and she and Ninyani were almost finished for the day. When they were done, they were planning to meet up with Dotty Marbles for a meal of street food before heading home together.

THE MANTIS CORRUPTION

At the end of the hallway, Auntie Peg approached a door and paused to make a note before entering. In the room, there were three patients all close to their ends. Over the previous 24 hours, each of them had displayed the final symptom of the blood corruption, and death always came not long after. Auntie Peg stepped up to each, dabbed the moisture from their brows and temples with a clean cloth, and she tucked their blankets tight.

Many of the city's inhabitants did not like to deal with a person afflicted by the blood corruption. When someone began to show signs of it, they were often sent straight to one of Teshon City's clinics for treatment. Auntie Peg possessed enough compassion for those stricken by the disease, to not only work at one of the clinics, but she ran it.

People feared the disease, but it was not contagious. Similar to different cancers, the blood corruption grew within an individual, potentially for years before it would manifest and run rampant through the body. The disease was often fatal, affecting children and the elderly quickest and most severely. It tended to linger in those who survived, causing minor issues for years after.

At any given time, there were between five and 20 patients under Auntie Peg's care. The staff who worked for her were devoted to the well-being of the sick, and she smiled when she heard the front door of the clinic open and the sound of her team's voices.

Ninyani stepped out of the room and called down the hall, "I'm finished reading!"

Auntie Peg waved for him to join her in her office, wrapped him in his shawl, and pulled on her jacket. They turned as the other healers came down the hallway.

"Right on time," Auntie Peg declared with a smile.

The night staff greeted her and Ninyani, and the two of them made their way out into the darkening city. Evening was slowly stealing the light as they walked together along a quiet city street. They turned onto one of the main thoroughfares, and ahead of them were a few shops with their lights still lit.

Dotty Marbles suddenly rounded a corner, saw Auntie Peg and Ninyani, and she rushed in their direction. She looked serious.

"What is it, sugar?" Auntie Peg asked as Dotty Marbles approached.

"Tchama didn't come see you two at the clinic, did she?"

Auntie Peg and Ninyani looked at each other.

"No, we haven't seen her. What happened?"

"You know the building with the warning signs behind the old Oselian warehouse in Gate Town?" Dotty Marbles asked. She was visibly shaken.

Auntie Peg and Ninyani nodded.

"Part of its wall fell and a little girl was almost killed. It was just dumb stupid luck that Tchama was standing next to her," Dotty Marbles declared. "She managed to shield the child with her body. It was a really horrible moment, until we all realized that they were both okay, but then Tchama wandered off, and she seemed really out of it."

"We haven't seen her," Ninyani stated. "Should we head over to the mystic's house and see if she's home now?"

"She's like me," Auntie Peg stated. "She can't have been injured."

Dotty Marbles furrowed her brow. "No, you're right. I don't think she was; I think she was upset. I don't know why. She saved that little girl."

"Tchama has struggled with the change that happened to her," Auntie Peg replied.

"She's been really sad since she lost her arm," Ninyani added in a quiet voice.

Auntie Peg and Dotty Marbles stood with Ninyani between them, and they both put an arm around their young friend as they headed through Gate Town.

"Her body may be strong right now," Auntie Peg explained, "but her spirit has been broken by what she went through. Also, coping with only having one arm has been frustrating for Tchama. You've been very compassionate, Ninyani," she added. "I don't know what could have made her distraught about saving someone."

The mystic's house was a little way from the clinic, and the trio talked as they walked. They soon arrived.

Dotty Marbles knocked on the front door and called out, "Tchama, are you home?"

They heard a noise on the other side, and Theolan opened the door. "Hello, lovely people," he exclaimed. "What a pleasant surprise!"

"Have you seen Tchama?" Ninyani asked him.

"I haven't," Theolan replied in alarm. "She's not here and hasn't come back from working with you earlier, Dot. Do you three want to come inside?"

"Oh, no, but thank you," Auntie Peg responded, "we're here uninvited, just wanted to check up on Tchama, but we'll leave you folks to your evening."

"Well, now I'm worried," Theolan declared.

"You needn't be, love," Auntie Peg said gently. "As you know, she's struggling with some things. She knows that your home is safe and welcoming, and she'll come back when she's ready."

Dotty Marbles added, "And thank you for providing her with that."

"Perhaps Tchama will pop by our place," Auntie Peg commented, "so, we ought to head there just in case."

Theolan gave them each air kisses and closed the door behind them.

"I hope she's okay," Ninyani said in a quiet voice★

Chapter 24 – Tchama & Olona

Tchama stepped up to the front door of the shop, pulled open the door, and its bell rang.

"Welcome to the First Organic Mechanic…" Olona started to say, but then she realized who it was. "Oh, hello! Tchama, I didn't expect to see you today, since you were helping with the…" Her voice faded.

Tchama was covered in dust and bits of concrete.

"What happened to you?" Olona asked.

Instead of replying, Tchama said, "I'm here to let you test my arm, or whatever you wanted to do."

Olona decided to leave her question for the moment. Tchama seemed very out of sorts. "Would you like a glass of water? Are you hungry? Have you been working all day?" Olona asked in quick succession.

"Water would be nice," Tchama replied.

Olona filled a glass from a pitcher and handed it to Tchama. She looked her over and said, "If you're up for it, we can test the strength of your grip again with a more substantial gauge, and then we can do the same thing with some of your other muscle groups."

Tchama nodded.

Olona laid out a few instruments, lit a joint, and began her experimentation. She took detailed notes, testing the strength of Tchama's individual fingers and several muscle groups in her arm and shoulder. Olona also spent a few moments determining the range of motion in Tchama's joints.

The testing did not last long, but it drifted by for Tchama like a haze. Since losing her arm, her spirit had darkened, and the method used to save her kept popping into her mind. Tchama's thoughts disturbed her. She knew that by consuming the photonova gland Ninyani brought with him from his village of Frostflower, she gained increased strength, but the near-invulnerable empowerment of her body felt like a curse.

It was not that Tchama was ungrateful to be alive, she was very grateful, but she could not help it that she felt like one of the hated Messiahs. The loss of her arm also weighed heavily on her soul, and the enthusiasm she once exuded had become almost extinguished.

Tchama was lost in her thoughts, and she wondered if she had been wrong in her thinking. She considered for the first time that it was possible what happened was a *good* thing. The mother of the little girl she saved certainly thought it was a good thing, and the woman did not react the way most people would have, learning that someone went through the Messiah enhancement; she was only appreciative that her child was safe.

Tchama spent most of the time since her enhancement wishing she did not go through with it, but for the first time, she began to feel grateful. Her dichotomous emotions were distracting her, and when Olona took her hand and stood there holding it, Tchama eventually made eye contact with her.

"What's wrong?" she asked.

Olona smiled. "I just said that we're all done. Are you sure you're all right? Do you want to tell me about anything? I could make us some food to..."

"I'm fine," Tchama replied. "I'm just going to head back to the mystic's house."

"Okay, well, thank you for coming by and letting me satisfy my curiosity," Olona said. "It was lovely meeting you yesterday, and you're most welcome to come visit me here at the shop anytime."

Tchama nodded and gave Olona a small smile. She made her way back out into the city streets, turned a corner, and entered Shifton. After a few minutes, she arrived at the home she shared with the mystic, his husband, and Lahari. Tchama entered, headed to the privy chamber, and she stripped off her dusty clothes.

She stepped under the overhead tap and cranked on the water. Tchama stood still for a long time with the falling water washing away the dust.

Emotions flooded and overwhelmed her in the moment, and she sobbed. She sobbed about almost dying a few months earlier; she sobbed over the loss of her arm, and she sobbed about needing assistance. Her tears flowed for the way she could not help but view herself as a cannibal. Tchama had also been feeling a noticeable loss of connection to Dozi and Ilya, and Tchama was heartbroken over it.

There was something else, though, something underneath her sadness, and it was breaking through to the surface. Tchama was feeling hope✪

Chapter 25 – Accepted

While Olona and Tisa were together at home and eating a late supper, the Biological Shift machine appeared in their kitchen.

"Tualu!" Tisa said in an excited voice. "Olona, it's Tualu!"

His unusual geometric form was limbless and headless. Made of unnatural metallic components and devices constructed by no human hand, Tualu was a sight to behold.

Olona, the organic mechanic, was amazed.

Tualu made no sound, but different pieces shifted and adjusted, creating the outline of a human handprint.

"He wants me to go with him," Tisa declared.

"Are you sure?" Olona replied.

"This is what happened last time." She rose from the table, stepped up to the Biological Shift in their kitchen, and said, "Hello, Tualu." She placed her palm on the handprint.

To Olona's surprise, Tisa and Tualu vanished.

The two of them reappeared in the basement chamber again where the other Biological Shifts were waiting. Tualu was beside Tisa.

"We'd like to officially welcome you to our little group, Tisa," Lahari stated. "We have a target, and this time, Tualu is confident in the team."

Tualu made no reply.

"Our intel is a little thin," S'Kay declared, "but we know that there are only Messiahs, so everyone we encounter is an enemy."

"Where are we going?" Tisa asked.

"After the battle of Gate Town, some of the surviving Messiahs fled to the Lesser Lighthouse. We need to eradicate them."

Tisa nodded. She looked determined.

"I think I have an idea," Gawa stated, and she looked Tisa up and down. "I don't want to put you at more risk than the rest of us, but I think you should be our distraction."

"What do you mean?" asked S'Kay.

"Yeah," Tisa interjected, "I can do more than just be a distraction."

Gawa continued, "We were wondering why Tualu brought someone who isn't a Bio-Shift into our team; I think it's because we need you. You can do something that none of us can." She looked at each of her unique companions. "Our appearances are too noticeable. We require surprise or stealth to attack, but Tisa," Gawa said, turning back to her, "you could walk right up to their front door."

Realization dawned on the others.

"If the Messiahs are distracted by you," Lahari said, "Tualu can teleport us inside the lighthouse, and we will be able to surprise them from within."

Tisa worried about the idea of going into this first battle isolated from the rest of the group, but she thought of the attack by the Demifae hunters in the alleyway. She hacked her way through all of them on her own. With her jaw set and her brow furrowed in determination, Tisa nodded at the others.

"Very well," Lahari concluded. "Tualu?"

He did not reply.

The others stepped up to him and each laid a hand against his mechanical body. They looked at Tisa, and as soon as her hand joined theirs, the group disappeared from the underground.

THE MANTIS CORRUPTION

Tisa manifested alone in the darkness. The blinking of the lesser lighthouse was ahead of her in the distance. She looked all around, but there was no sign of the Biological Shifts. A barricade of debris stretched across the peninsula, and as she approached, she drew the attention of the Messiahs.

Tisa shouted lines that she had spoken before.

"I can hear the cosmic music from the radiation of the universe! I can taste the elements that burn in the stars! I can see the world; I can see eons! I look into distant corners of alien galaxies!"

As she began to repeat herself, her words gained the reaction she expected.

"I can hear the cosmic music from the radiation of the universe!"

Curious Messiahs came out of the lighthouse to see who was yelling.

Tisa screamed her words at the sight of them.

"I can taste the elements that burn in the stars!" and the Messiahs were met with devastation.

Pockets of darkness opened around the oncoming enemies. However, as they swatted at them as if they were no more than irritating insects, the Messiahs shrieked in agony. One man's arm was lopped off, went spinning through the air, and it landed on the pavement with a wet flub. Another was hacked along the outside of his hand, and he lost three of his fingers and a massive chunk of his forearm. Both men's blood gushed from the horrible wounds, and their cries of anguish drew other Messiahs to the front of the lighthouse.

"I can see the world; I can see eons!"

Tisa raged her words at them, words that her missing friend used to say. Tilby's words inspired the phrases that flowed from her lips. She continued her onslaught, as countless entities appeared from the disks she created around her enemies.

"I look into distant corners of alien galaxies!"

Messiahs rushed at Tisa, but suddenly all her shadow disks disappeared and a large void opened between her and the Messiahs. A geyser of black radiation erupted and blasted through the barricade, boring into four more Messiahs. Two of them caught the beam square in their torsos, and it punched holes through their chests wider than a grapefruit. Tisa's assault collided with one

Messiah in his hip, and his entire leg dropped to the stones. He fell beside it, screaming and squirming in horrible pain.

The third Messiah was grazed by Tisa's blast, and his body was sent spinning. He tumbled beside his fallen companions, pushed himself up, and another disk of darkness appeared before him. From it protruded massive jagged spikes like teeth and a serpentine tongue that wrapped around the man's neck. The Messiah tried to grab it and pull himself free, but the disc closed over him like a mouth. His head and hands disappeared and a trio of blood geysers sprayed into the air.

In the short time it took Tisa to reach the ruined barricade, there was already an enormous pool of Messiah blood in front of the lighthouse, and no other Messiahs exited the structure as she approached. Tisa could hear screams coming from within, and she raced inside to help. It sounded like the Biological Shifts were already tangled with more Messiahs.

Tisa found a set of stairs that led up to the light, and down to whatever basement was beneath the lighthouse. That was where the voices were coming from, and she raced down toward them.

After Tualu left Tisa alone outside the lighthouse, he brought the others into a storeroom in the cellars. They could hear voices shouting that the lighthouse was under attack, and the Biological Shifts rushed out to surprise anyone they would encounter.

The doors of another chamber swung open, and the two groups were face-to-face. The Messiahs were shocked by the Biological Shifts. They appeared monstrous to the Messiahs, who staggered back.

The warriors attacked.

Gawa poured her terrible violet electricity through her hands into the first two Messiahs that she grabbed.

S'Kay's feathers bit into Messiahs' empowered flesh, liquefying their skin and muscles from their bones, leaving them green and hideous.

Ijeron's body split apart like liquid mercury, and his projectiles pierced multiple Messiahs before he again coalesced.

Lahari was like a whirlpool of terror. She walked into the Messiahs' midst and devoured their energies with ruthless devastation.

Khano roared like the bear-man he was, and he unleashed a pair of blue beams from his eyes. They cut through a Messiah, who crashed to the stone floor, dead.

Yxida stayed behind the others, creating weapons out of everything that surrounded the Messiahs. Barrels and crates changed their molecular structure and she reconfigured them into swords and spears with unnatural density that were able to injure even the empowered Messiahs. Yxida caused a chunk of wall to become a whirling blade that went spinning through the air and cut deep into one enemy's neck.

Without warning, a disk of shadow appeared in the middle of the fighting, and from it rose a monster. The creature bore a resemblance to a mythological dragon, and its onslaught was terrible. A pair of Messiahs caught the creature's claws in their chests, and the gashes it ripped were gruesome. The thing also reared forward and sank its teeth into a third Messiah, biting through the man's shoulder and upper chest. He wailed in pain that was hitherto unimagined and fell away from the beast with his arm wagging uselessly, barely still attached.

The dragon vanished and six new discs appeared surrounding another Messiah. Out of them thrust spikes that struck like lightning, piercing multiple holes in the man's torso. He fell down dead.

"Those are Tisa's disks," Lahari proclaimed. "She's killing Messiahs and she's not even in here with us!" Lahari released a withered body, which fell wheezing to the floor.

Tisa stepped through the doorframe at the top of the stairs, as the last Messiahs were dying.

The basement chamber was strewn with corpses in a variety of strange states. A few were charred husks of themselves with little bolts of lavender lightning dancing across their frames. Several bodies were in various stages of being melted. A number of Messiahs bore holes punched through their torsos, and quite a few miscellaneous limbs lay beside the bodies from which they were cleaved.

"Through a window upstairs," Tisa told the others, "I saw a group of Messiahs jump from the cliffs into Teshon Harbor."

"There will always be more Messiahs out there that need murdering," Lahari stated.

"I want to do it again," Tisa declared, "and I want to do it again soon."★

Chapter 26 – Ronging, Part Four

Ronging's slow trudge led him away from Tuilii la Ru and out across the rolling grasslands of Xin. It took him many long days of travel, but they were uneventful, and he eventually arrived at the edge of Gunge.

On those rare occurrences over the years when his addiction flared up and he left the familiarity of Gunge to hunt, Ronging missed neither his home nor any of the other inhabitants. Happiness, contentment, peace, joy, these were all former emotions that were no longer entertained by Ronging or any other mutated Messiah. However, the scene that awaited Ronging shocked even *his* emotionless mind. He froze and stared.

Down in the valley, there was no movement. It was not that none of his kin was visible, he could see their bodies; none was left alive.

Not a single inhabitant of Gunge remained, and Ronging howled at the sky like a beast. He collapsed to the earth and fell silent.

"*Ronging!*" roared a voice that he recognized. "I have returned from Teshon City!"✪

Chapter 27 – Gunge, Part Two

The sun was beaming down and a sea breeze was blowing across the valley home of the twisted monsters that used to be human, and the creatures of Gunge stirred en masse.

"Food," one of them murmured.

"Smell it," another hissed.

"*Look!*" screeched a multi-mouthed mutated Messiah, and it pointed with all five of its arms toward the ridge above the ravine.

Limbs flexed, and the beasts began to propel themselves up the hill. Each monster moved in its own unique manner. Too many arms and legs forced several of them to slither, while many others crawled. Only a few managed a semblance of walking.

Up on the ridge, Lahari smirked. "They know we're here," she declared. Everything about her was vicious.

Beside her, Gawa's patterned skin pulsed with her energies.

S'Kay flexed, and her feathers rippled.

Tualu was not with them, but the newer members were.

Ijeron's reflective skin shone brilliantly in the unhindered sunlight.

The bear-man, Khano, was standing motionless. A low growl rumbled from his throat and blue energy crackled in his eyes.

Yxida and Tisa stood side by side. Yxida looked up at Tisa, who looked back down at her new friend. After the attack on the Lesser Lighthouse, the Biological Shifts brought Tisa to Red Ravens in celebration. She and Yxida became fast friends. They now smiled at each other with wicked grins, before turning their gaze back toward the monsters.

The ridge above the creatures looked like it was lined with warrior gods and goddesses. If the mutated Messiahs still possessed the capacity to fear, they would have been terrified.

There were two other individuals with the Biological Shifts and Tisa. Olona and Tchama were standing on the land's rise, and they were poised for battle. Tchama was smiling like she had not smiled since she lost her arm, and *something* now replaced it.

Olona did not look like Olona. Her body was much more mechanical than normal. Many small devices were attached all over her.

Tchama balled her hand into a fist, and she looked down at the thing that now took up the space of her former arm. It looked nothing like an arm; it was a weapon. Tchama turned to Olona with a beaming smile.

"I can't tell you how much I appreciate what you've done for me," she exclaimed. "You've helped me feel whole again in a way I didn't expect. I feel like myself again. No," she paused and corrected, "I feel like so much *more* than myself!"

Lahari spoke over her. "That's nice and all, but this really isn't the time. Each of us is impressed with your new arm."

"Sorry there's no way to make you an actual replacement arm," Olona whispered to Tchama, "but let me know how that battle prosthetic feels against the Gungites. You should've seen what it took to sharpen the high-density blade," she added, "and I managed to make the bludgeon so dense that when I was done with it, I couldn't lift the thing!"

The weapon that was now attached to Tchama's shoulder matched her other arm in size, and it bent for her at the elbow and wrist like her real arm, but that was the extent of the similarities. It was not shaped like a human arm, and it did not have fingers at the end of it. Instead, a double-edged battle-axe the size of a large dinner plate graced the place where her hand would have been, and it was not the weapon's only blade.

Olona continued whispering. "The limb's joints are calibrated to match the strength of your arm, and the materials should be equally as durable. Sorry," she repeated, "that there's no way to make you a new arm."

"They're getting closer," Lahari stated in a voice that insisted Tchama and Olona stop discussing things.

"I love it!" Tchama said under her breath back to Olona.

Olona could not have looked prouder. "The designs for the minor protrusions all over the outer side of the limb are based on S'Kay's arm-feathers." Olona turned to Tisa. "Thanks for introducing me to everyone after your attack on the lighthouse."

None of the others were listening. Tisa, S'Kay, and the others were focused on the enemies.

Tchama took Olona's hand. "How do I switch the weapon?" she asked.

"Oh, turn the axe widdershins," Olona instructed, "and it'll flip outwards."

Tchama twisted the blade and it folded in half and inserted itself into the limb. A long metal pole with a bulbous knob on its end extended from the fingerless hand. It was fused in place, but with the flexibility of the limb's wrist joint, Tchama wielded the bludgeon like a wicked club.

"It's perfect," Tchama declared. She switched the weapon back to its axe.

Lahari growled, "Enough talking."

To everyone's surprise, Tisa suddenly screamed like a banshee. She raced toward the oncoming horde surrounded by many of her voids in the atmosphere. They launched forward in front of her and manifested monsters of shadow and smoke, like creatures from the deep. Eyeless faces of teeth and tentacles, fleshy limbs with claws and strange probing fingers, eldritch entities reached out in darkness toward the mutated Messiahs.

"Tisa's leading the charge! *On her!*" Lahari ordered, and her troop's battle cry was terrific. They descended.

Olona brought one palm to her opposite forearm, pointed two fingers at the nearest monstrosity, and she unleashed a bolt of white-hot lightning. It burned through the creature, and the bolt leapt, ripping into two more of them.

Tchama used her empowered legs, leaping high into the air above the other warriors' heads, and she came crashing down on one of the mutated horde. She brought her new mechanic organic battle prosthetic down with the force of an avalanche, and Tchama's blow hit the nigh-invincible monstrosity and it ruptured like an overripe tomato. The thing's innards burst out across the hillside, and it shrieked, writhing on the ground with its many arms and legs thrashing. Two tongues lolled out of its weird mouth, and its head rocked back and forth in agony.

Tchama was covered in its blood and slime.

Lahari gave her an admiring glance.

Tchama's face wore an expression of glee. She reached down, gripped one of the monster's seizing limbs, and she spun her body around in a graceful rotation. The creature was yanked from the ground by Tchama's strength, and she released it, hurtling it through the air into another of its twisted kind and knocking it back. A trail of guts stretched between her and the beasts, and the other monster rose in a fury.

It pounced toward Tchama, but Tisa's shadows appeared and enveloped the thing in midair. Its body ruptured and the pieces hit the ground, so many pieces, far too many different body parts for a single human being.

S'Kay fought in an almost bird-like manner, darting from one enemy to another. She leapt over them and nicked their flesh with her brutal feathers. The monsters roared with their strange voices, as the places she touched began to disintegrate and drip to the ground. The creatures watched their own body parts melting.

Gawa's cosmic electricity radiated out from her. She glowed purple, and the patterns on her skin ripped across her epidermis like unearthly waves. As the monsters approached to attack her, blasts of her energy discharged and sent each enemy flying backward. Their bodies bore scorched patches that crackled and ate into them, and with curiosity, their fellow creatures watch them dying.

The Biological Shifts and Tisa, with Tchama and Olona, reigned fury down upon their remaining enemies.

The beasts wailed in rage and redoubled their assault on the invaders of Gunge.

A pair of them lumbered toward Lahari, but they were no match for her black hole of power. It ripped into them, and they screamed, as their bodies began to shrink. Lahari grabbed them as they tried to pull away, and she gripped both tight. Other monsters saw her devastation of their kind, and they backed away from the scaly blue-skinned woman with the halo of black spines surrounding her face.

From behind the battle, a thin beam of energy cut through the air. It hit a monster in the forehead, and the thing stopped cold.

Olona laughed aloud from her ranged position. "That got it!" She blew smoke from an opening in the back of her wrist. "Reloading!" she called out as she pushed a button on her forearm. "Aiming."

The creature she shot collapsed to the ground, and Olona fired a second blast that was also right on target with another monster. Her beam hit it in the shoulder and it squealed like a hog, as one of its many arms fell to the ground.

"That can't feel good," Olona laughed.

"I'll say," Lahari called up to her, as the two monsters she still held continued to diminish in size. "What is that weapon?"

Olona looked proud. "I call this one a luminous beam. I designed it based on Harakin's power. It's strong enough to pierce nine inches of Oselian steel plating, you know, the really hard stuff. It can get through *nine* of them before running out of energy." She sounded amazed. "I suspect that dead one has a hole burned straight through it." Olona continued, "But I don't think I hit anything vital in its friend."

Blood was pouring from where the thing's arm used to be.

"Reloading!" Olona sang aloud.

Ijeron's body split, and he sent his projectiles into the monster Olona had wounded. The thing momentarily froze, then it twisted into an even more bizarre shape, before Ijeron's pieces exited in many different directions. The monster's corpse crumpled to the earth.

Lahari released her grip on the two victims she had absorbed, but to her surprise, a man and a woman were looking back at her. Both of them were naked.

"Who the fuck are you?" Lahari asked, and she shoved them away from her.

They fell onto the grass and both looked very confused.

"We're not..." the woman started to say, "monsters anymore?" but neither of them was given an opportunity to reflect further on their renewed condition.

A disc of Tisa's shadow appeared in front of Lahari, and from it came an enormous serpentine neck, and the thing's head was only mouth. It chomped down, biting off the top half of the man and the woman. Their waists and legs quivered where they knelt for a moment, as if yet to realize they were no longer attached to bodies, and they slumped to the earth.

"Huh," Lahari mused, "my power seemed to revert them back to their human forms." She laughed. "They didn't stand a chance against you, Tisa!"

Khano was bigger than any of the mutated Messiahs, and he wrestled them with his bear-like strength. He also possessed other physiological advantages over his fleshy enemies, and his claws and teeth eviscerated whichever of the monsters dared to challenge him. Khano's other ability made him even more brutal. He used the blue beams from his eyes strategically, blasting hideous holes into the Messiahs' flesh while he fought with them.

Yxida let out a powerful battle cry. The short woman raised her hands above her horned head, and one of the monsters stopped dead in its tracks. Its many limbs pulled against its body like a dying insect, and it screamed and fell silent. Yxida began converting its very matter into sand, and it started to pour onto the ground. The creature squirmed, inadvertently shaking more of its body free as the tiny particles. A moment later, there was nothing left of the beast.

Olona fired a final beam of piercing energy that cut into one of the monster's torsos. "I'm out!" she yelled, and she sounded delighted. "Commencing close-range attack!" she declared, and she rushed down the hill over the many dead Messiahs.

Tisa cried out. "Olona! You're just a human…" but her words disappeared.

Olona pushed another button, and a glow of energy surrounded her body like a second skin. She ran into the nearest oncoming creature, and it flailed at her, but its limbs hit her protective radiation shield with a horrible sizzle. It wailed in pain as it tried to pull its scorched body away from her.

"Oh, no you don't!" Olona snapped, and she jumped onto the monster. She grabbed one of its many arms and wrapped hers around its neck.

The creature let out an ear-splitting noise, and it began to convulse, but Olona held it fast. It shook beneath her for a moment, then collapsed to the hillside and stopped moving. A few residual twitches rippled through it, and Olona's shield killed the thing.

"Wow," Tisa said.

The battle raged.

Tchama stowed the axe head, and the bludgeon extended. She gripped the base of the club where it attached to the end of the organic mechanic limb, and with a double-handed grip, she swung it at the monsters with devastating results.

Khano body-checked a monster toward Tchama, and her club collided with its head. There was a loud and unnerving pop, and the thing's neck was broken. It slumped to the hillside, and Tchama roared as she raised her weapon overhead and brought it down. The beast's blood sprayed up on Tchama, and Khano let out a deep chuckle at her brutality.

Lahari was busy turning another monster back into a mere human, as Yxida and Ijeron slayed the final two remaining beasts. The hillside was covered in gore, as Lahari released another naked man from her grip, and he fell to the slime.

He tried to push himself up, but a pair of blue beams pierced straight through his heart. He collapsed and did not move again.

Only the warriors remained.

"Well, that was an overwhelming success," Olona commented. She put her hand on Gawa's patterned shoulder, and the Biological Shift woman flinched slightly at the touch. "You really are amazing," Olona marveled at them, "each one of you!"

Gawa looked surprised, and she stared at Olona with her blank white eyes. "You don't think it's, I don't know, gross to touch me?"

Olona looked hurt, but not by Gawa's words. It was as if even the very idea that Gawa, or any of the Biological Shifts, felt untouchable, hurt Olona. "I'm so sorry," she blurted out, quickly removing her hand from Gawa's shoulder. "I should not have just reached out and touched you. I apologize." She then asked, "May I please touch your arm again?"

Gawa was confused and turned her gaze to the others. "I guess so," she replied with an uncertain shrug.

Surrounded by the gore of the destroyed monsters, Olona returned her palm to Gawa's skin. "I don't think you're gross at all."★

Chapter 28 – Ronging & the Other

A monster was approaching Ronging. He recognized it but did not know what name it called itself. The existence of mutated Messiahs did not include a need for them to remember the details of their kind, but Ronging inherently knew the other creature was one of them.

It spoke in a strange voice and knew his name. "Ronging, I have returned from Teshon City."

Ronging looked over the gory hillside, covered in the many corpses and body parts.

"They're all dead?" the other monster asked. "All dead," it repeated in a growl. "Ronging, come with me," the creature commanded.

Ronging turned and faced his fellow beast. Only one monster of Gunge wore anything on its twisted body, and that weird individual was now before him. It did not wear clothes, but on its head was a mechanical crown.✪

Chapter 29 – The Market

From the front door of the mystic's house came a cheery knock.

"That must be Olona and Tisa!" Tchama declared to the others in a bright voice. The sash she was wearing around her neck that draped over the stump of her shoulder was made of shimmering gold and silver fabric. Tchama turned the handle, and sure enough, the two women were on the other side of the door.

"Hello!" the mystic called to them with a wave. "Everyone, let's head outside."

He and Tchama stepped out into the morning sunshine with Lahari behind them. S'Kay, Gawa, Ijeron, and Yxida followed, and the mystic locked the door.

Tisa leaned down and gave Yxida a peck on her cheek.

"G'morning," Yxida exclaimed to her and Olona.

"Hi!" Olona replied. She stepped around Tisa and wrapped Lahari in an unexpected hug.

"Oh," Lahari said in surprise, "erm... hello."

Olona stepped back with a beaming smile. "Good morning!"

Lahari seemed unsure of the physical contact, but Tisa giggled at Olona's enthusiasm.

Theolan came around from the back of the house, holding Khano's huge paw. "What a fascinating story!" he said up to the bear-man. "Thank you for telling me about your past, and I'd love to hear more about what you've gone through someday, whenever you're up for sharing more."

Khano sniffed hard and dapped his eye with a dainty handkerchief. "Thanks," he said in a gentle growl.

Theolan squeezed his paw and turned to the others. "This way!" he called. "The market's not far. Come along!" He continued holding Khano's paw as they all headed on their way.

S'Kay stepped up to Olona and walked beside her. "So, what's your fascination with us Bio-Shifts?" but Tisa responded to her instead.

"Olona is one of the most accepting people," she said, "and she's very curious."

Olona grinned awkwardly and a little blush worked its way up her cheeks. "Yeah, I don't know, S'Kay. Down in Xin, where we're from," she said, indicating herself and Tisa, "Shifts aren't talked about. I didn't know any Shift people, and I didn't know Bio-Shifts, like all of you, even existed. And Tisa's right," Olona added with an embarrassed smile, "my curiosity sometimes gets the better of me."

Tisa added, "Olona has always been positive about my powers. S'Kay, the word you used was perfect; she has a strong sense of *fascination* about the world."

The blush on Olona's cheeks darkened and she brought her hand to the back of her neck. "I love diversity," Olona said, "and there wasn't much of it in Xin." She took S'Kay's hand. "The things that Shifts can do are astonishing!"

"We're almost at the market," Tchama declared. She was beaming and skipping along around the group, and her renewed joy warmed the mystic's heart.

S'Kay took her hand back from Olona, but then she realized that she had liked the feeling of their hands together.

"So, now that the monsters of Gunge have all been slaughtered, do you think people will make the journey to Xin?" the mystic asked.

Olona perked up. "Tisa," she said, "you haven't told them yet?" However, before Tisa could reply, Olona continued in an excited voice. "We want to lead expeditions between the two! Tisa and I are planning to offer guided services back and forth between Xin and Teshon City."

The murmur from a boisterous crowd began to grow as the group approached the Shifton outdoor market.

"The mountains were rugged," Tisa added, "but we made it, and now there's no monsters to murder anyone at the border of Xin, so maybe people will want to make the journey."

"I think it will be a good source of income," Olona added.

"That is quite an idea," the mystic said to Tisa and Olona.

"There they are!" Tchama blurted out with an excited laugh. She pointed through the other shoppers at a table of mushrooms.

Dozi was surprised to see them. "What are all of you doing here?" she asked. Harakin and Sumi were behind the table with her.

The mystic, Theolan, Lahari, Tchama, S'Kay, Gawa, Ijeron, Yxida, Khano, Tisa, and Olona crowded around the front of Dozi's table.

"We just wanted to come see you!" the mystic declared. "Good morning, Dozi!" He beamed at her.

"*Ahem!*" coughed an annoyed voice behind everyone, but then they heard a giggle that they recognized, and the voice added in a dramatic tone, "Wish this ragtag bunch of ragamuffins would shift it, so I can get some 'shrooms!" and everyone turned around to see the smiling faces of Auntie Peg and Ninyani.

"Look at all of you!" Ninyani cried out in delight. He ran up and hugged Tchama. "I love your drape," he cooed, stroking the fabric that covered her missing arm.

"And don't you just look adorable?" Tchama replied.

Ninyani was wearing fitted animal print leggings and a flouncy tank top, and his hair was wrapped in a silky scarf.

"Would you get out of my way?!" Auntie Peg joked, pushing through her large group of friends to Dozi's table.

"So, why are all of you here?" Ninyani asked Tchama.

She gave him a one-armed squeeze. "Because we just wanted to see who we'd run into! We wanted to come say *hi* to Dozi, and we hoped you three might be here, too. Hey, where's Dot?"

Ninyani pointed across the market. "She's right there," he replied, "getting bacon for breakfast tomorrow."

Dotty Marbles was laughing with another vendor.

"I'm gonna grab a coffee," Gawa informed the others. Theolan, Ijeron, Yxida, and Tisa all joined her and headed toward the rich aroma.

Dotty Marbles had not noticed any of them, and Ijeron disconnected one of his hands at the wrist. It sailed through the air with his fingers extended, and his open palm slapped right into Dotty Marbles' backside.

She squealed and jumped and spun around with a mischievous smile on her face, but then she looked confused, as she realized that no one was behind her.

Ijeron's silver hand floated up and waved.

Dotty Marbles immediately understood, and she looked past the hand, scanning the crowd for the people she called friends.

Ijeron's hand pointed for her, and she smiled wide as the group appeared among the shoppers. His hand zipped back to him and reattached.

"Hey there, sleazies!" Dotty Marbles called out to them.

Theolan trotted over and hugged her. "Hey, gurl!" he said and gave her a peck on the cheek.

"Dot, would you want a coffee, too?" Tisa offered.

"Oh-ho, no, thank you!" Dotty Marbles replied with a laugh. "Peggy makes stronger coffee than you're likely to find here, and I've already had two cups this morning." She made a silly face, and Ninyani and Tchama laughed.

They stepped up to the coffee cart as Dotty Marbles headed toward Dozi's mushroom table. As she approached the mystic, she gave his round bottom a playful pinch.

"Oooh!" he cried out in surprise. "Dot, you scamp!"

She leaned down and planted an affectionate kiss on his cheek, leaving a red lipstick mark.

Dotty Marbles was taller than everyone in their group except Khano, but she looked around, confused not to see the other tall person she expected. "Hey, where's Ilya?" she asked the others.

Ilya was not behind the booth with Dozi, Harakin, and Sumi.

"She's in the forest," Dozi replied, as she packed up Auntie Peg's purchases. "She flew up last night and usually spends a few days away in nature."

"Wow, that's incredible," Dotty Marbles replied. "And I love how nonchalantly we all talk about the Shifts who are our friends, as if their powers aren't the most wondrous things on earth!" Dotty Marbles affected her voice with an amusing impression of Dozi and said, "Ilya flew away, no big deal," then she finished in her regular voice, "as if someone *flying* is the most normal thing ever," and she laughed.★

Chapter 30 – Olona & Sumi

Olona jumped up when the bell to the front door of her shop rang, and she greeted her guest.

"Good morning, Sumi," she said. "Thanks so much for coming by, and thanks again for loaning me your file for the past week. It was a fascinating read! I'm excited to see what we can find out."

Sumi looked unsure. "You read it? You mean, you actually understood it? What do you want me to do?" she asked.

Olona smiled. "Come in and we can try a few things. Let's go into the back room where I've got some gear set up. Would you like a cup of tea?"

"No, thank you," Sumi replied as they headed through the storefront.

"Alright," Olona said, "then if you're ready, let's get started. First, can I simply observe you using your powers? Will you please just go from one side of the room to the other in front of me?"

"Okay," Sumi replied, and suddenly she was standing on the other side of the room.

"Wow," Olona whispered. "That's incredible! Do you mind telling me what you experience when you use your powers, while I put something together?" She waved at her organic mechanic equipment, lit a joint, and sat at her table to assemble a few small components.

Sumi explained, "I refer to them as doorways. It feels like they open on my skin, and then I can move through them. The doorways lead me from one place to another."

Olona looked up at her. "What happens if you just open a doorway and feel it on your skin, like you said, but then you don't go through it?" She continued manipulating the instrument she was constructing.

"I've never done that. I just go through when it's there."

Olona made a note and requested of Sumi, "Next, can you teleport me across the room with you?"

Sumi nodded. "Yes," she said, and she held out her hand.

Olona reached up from her seat at the table, took Sumi's hand, and suddenly they were both on the other side of the room. Olona was still in a seated position but the chair was no longer beneath her. Her hand slipped from Sumi's, and Olona's backside hit the floor.

"*Oooff!*"

Sumi looked mortified. "Oh, I'm so sorry! I should've made you stand up first!"

Olona laughed. "No, no," she replied, as she rose to her feet, "that was unbelievable, marvelous! I don't even know what I just experienced," she exclaimed in a delighted voice. "How long did you feel the doorway open before you took my hand?"

"I don't know what you mean," Sumi responded.

Olona concentrated, trying to organize her words. "I guess I'm asking if you felt the doorway open at the same instant that our hands touched, or was it already open, and *then* you grabbed my hand?"

Sumi seemed to ponder Olona's words. "Well, no, my doorway doesn't appear at the same instant. It's more like it's waiting for me."

Olona stepped up to the table and lifted the device she constructed. "Can you take me across the room again," she asked, "but this time, please hold this in your hand?"

"Okay," Sumi agreed.

She took Olona's small machine, but Olona pulled her hand away and quickly asked, "Can you feel your doorway?"

Sumi hesitated. "Yes," she said with uncertainty in her voice.

"Look through it, but don't step through it," Olona instructed. "Can you still feel it?"

"I can." Sumi closed her eyes and gasped. "I can see you from the other side of the room! *I can see myself!*"

"Yes! That's perfect." Olona was very pleased with the results. "Can you step through it and keep it open?"

Sumi opened her eyes. "What do you mean?"

"Can you teleport to the other side of the room, but when you arrive, can you feel the same way that you feel right now? Can you go through and still *feel* the doorway?"

Sumi concentrated and appeared on the other side of the room.

"Close your eyes!" Olona quickly instructed. "Can you still see me?"

"It's gone," Sumi said in a disappointed tone.

"No problem, that's no problem at all," Olona replied. "These are all just tests. I want to make a few notes. Will you teleport across the room several times so that the device can take some readings?"

"Okay," Sumi said, and she extended the little machine back to Olona. "Here you go."

Olona looked confused. "It needs you to teleport in order to take the readings."

Sumi furrowed her brow. "I just did," she responded. "I went back and forth nine times. You didn't..." she hesitated. "You didn't see me?"

Olona tentatively took the device from Sumi's hand. To her surprise, sure enough, it was registered with nine teleportations in less than a nanosecond.

"Wow," Olona whispered again. "Can you do it one more time, just across the room?"

Sumi obliged and took back the device. She stepped through another doorway and appeared across the room.

"Thank you," Olona said, and she began to write furiously into a large bound notebook.

Sumi stood there awkwardly holding the device for several minutes.

Olona repeated herself when she finished making her notes. "Thank you. May I please see the final reading?"

Sumi returned the device to Olona, who plugged it into the cable from the organic mechanic device in her forearm.

"Wow, this data is unbelievable." She looked Sumi in the eyes. "Your file states that it's possible for you to see through your doorways, like we just proved, but it also says that you can go into and remain in that in-between space before teleporting out again."

Sumi did not respond and seemed uncertain.

"Do you want to see if you can teleport across the room," Olona suggested, "but not immediately? What if you open another doorway, and peer through it, but then you just enter it without exiting on the other side."

"That doesn't seem possible," Sumi replied.

"If they put it in your file," Olona commented, "that makes me think they tested and were able to prove these details about your powers." Olona furrowed her brow. "But, Sumi, I don't want you to feel the way you did back at the compound. I don't want you to feel like I'm running experiments on you to hurt you. Those people kept a lot of facts hidden from you about your powers, but *I* want you to know everything you can about yourself. You are truly incredible, Sumi. I'm in awe of you."

Sumi could not help but blush a little. "This doesn't feel like the compound at all," she said quietly. "The medics were horrible and the officers were worse."

"Well, I do *not* want you to feel what you felt with them, not with me," Olona stated. "If I suggest a test that you don't want to do, just let me know. Also, if you ever want to tell me what happened to you, I know that I'm not even 20 yet, but I think I'm a pretty good listener. Conversely," Olona added, "if you *never* want to think about those things again, we don't ever have to discuss them."

Sumi had been in Teshon City for less than a month, but she had already experienced an abundance of compassion and understanding from the people with whom she and Harakin had become friends. She gave Olona a steadfast look. "I'm interested in seeing what we can figure out, what they wanted to keep from me."

Olona beamed at her and replied, "Not only are you powerful, but since knowledge is power," she declared, "learning about yourself makes you even more powerful!"

Sumi smiled. "Okay, let me try and see if I can go in between without going all the way through my doorway." She closed her eyes and said, "I can see us from the other side of the room again."

"Good, it came naturally that time. What if you continue to look through your doorway after you step in, but don't stop looking through, will that keep you in between?"

Sumi disappeared.

Olona looked around and headed out into the front area of her shop. "Sumi?" she called to the empty space.

To Olona's surprise, Sumi suddenly reappeared in the backroom with a small girl, and they both fell to the floor.

Olona rushed over to help Sumi up, and both of them spoke in unison.

Olona asked, "*Who is this?*" at the same instant Sumi gasped, "*The princess?!*"

The young child groaned, sat up, and stared at Sumi and Olona.

The two women looked at each other and then back at the girl.

"How are you alive?" Sumi whispered in shock.

"Are you okay?" Olona asked the child.

"I was in the castle," the princess whimpered, "and everyone was dying." Tears poured from her eyes.

Olona tried to comfort her. "You're okay. You're safe now. No one is going to hurt you." She put an arm around the girl. "Would you like something to eat or drink?" she offered.

The princess sniffed hard and wiped her eyes. "No, I'm not hungry. We just finished breakfast, and I'm still full."

The bell at the front door of Olona's shop rang again, and Ilya's voice suddenly cried out, "*Olona!* Where are you, Olona?!"

"I'm back here with Sumi!" she replied.

Ilya burst in urgently. She ignored Sumi and the young girl who she did not recognize, and Ilya looked right at Olona.

"I need your help!" ✪

- Book 4 is now available!
"The Mantis Continuum"

172

Adam Andrews Johnson

173